Yesterdays Legacy

Ann McGowan

Yesterdays Legacy now available from:
Choice Publishing Online Bookstore @ www.choicepublishing.ie
Amazon.co.uk and other leading online bookstores.

Dedicated, with my love, to my children and grandchildren.
The people who make my life worthwhile

Author's Note

All through my life reading and writing have been very important. My imagination takes over and I am in another world. My children say if I hadn't got a book to read the label on the sauce bottle would do. I claim if I didn't write I would have gone insane long ago, although there is an entrenched belief in some that I am mad already! This has yet to be confirmed.

Over the years I have had many short stories, articles and poetry published. It was my way of escaping from reality when rearing my children. It changes my thought process and mood by developing ideas and fantasies.

Born and brought up in the Border town of Ballyshannon, Co Donegal, most of my life I have heard stories of 'The Troubles'. I spent a lot of my 'ill spent youth' around The Falls Rd and Andersonstown, Belfast. I lived in Strabane for four years in the early 70s and have many relatives and friends living in Northern Ireland. I also know many who left their homes in Northern Ireland to live 'across the Border'. All this has had a big influence on my thinking and I developed an affinity with the Catholics in the North and an empathy with them against the discrimination and hardships they had to endure.

After I heard a chance remark

"There are only lowlife thugs in the IRA" and having a fertile imagination I thought

"Wouldn't it make a good story if I depicted the main characters as middle class IRA running a covert IRA unit and especially if one of those was a woman"

I started to write the story and it took on a life of its own. I added to it as time went by when I heard or read snippets that I could develop. I would then leave it until I heard something else. Over the years it grew to what it is today.

You now have the finished article in your hands, I hope you enjoy it.

Author's Biography

Ann Mc Gowan went back to education in her forties and graduated from Queen's University in Community Drama, UCD in Women in Politics and the Economy and UNI Galway in Community Development and Peace Building. She has also completed training in Management, Training the Trainer, Media Studies, Women in Leadership, Advanced Facilitation, Human Resources
She is a Project Coordinator in a Community Development in her home town working to promote inclusion and combat poverty. She is the mother of four children and five granddaughters

Introduction

Colly could never be called conventional. She was always a rebel but she gave the impression that 'butter wouldn't melt in her mouth'.

When she, Chris, Pat and Tom got together it was a recipe for trouble. All were intent on doing their bit for Ireland with a determination to make a difference. Together they ran one of the most covert and successful units of the IRA. No one was privy to their secret, except one IRA commander and even he did not know all the names of the members. There was very little chance of betrayal. They were comrades and friends for almost thirty years and nothing could divide them.

None of Colly's family and friends knew of her other life and she often wondered what they would say if they knew of her clandestine activities and the mayhem she often left in her wake as she travelled around Northern Ireland in her smart business suit, perfect make up, stiletto heels and carrying her briefcase. A briefcase like no other!

But no matter what you believe, circumstances change and time goes on and you also change. You have to question your methods and sometimes your motives. But do you or can you?

Yesterdays Legacy

By

Ann Mc Gowan

Printed by Choice Publishing

Drogheda, Co Louth

November 2009

Chapter One

She stared out the window while rivulets of rain cascaded down the panes of glass creating a kaleidoscope of colour from the flowers in the garden. From outside the window yellow, orange, red, blue and white mingled together, creating a profusion of multicoloured designs in each square pane.

Colly noticed none of this, her brain felt as though it was being squeezed tight to the size of a golf ball and at any moment now she expected it to explode. She was terrified. Intermittently flashbacks of her life sprang from this terror reminding her of who she was, where she'd been and how she got to where she was today.

She could see clearly, as though on a movie reel, how her thoughts and actions had been shaped and dictated by all those she came into contact with, what she had experienced, what she believed or had chosen to believe from those she had met along the way, and what she had heard or read. The good and the bad, all shaping the journey that brought her to this moment!

Now she was looking back at her life as though it belonged to another person. Where had all those years gone? She could pinpoint every milestone along the way as though they were surrounded by neon lights. Although the story felt as if it belonged to someone else, she knew that she alone had made the choices and no one else was to blame for the outcome except herself. She had taken from each person and event what she wanted. She had made the decisions and until this moment had never regretted one of them.

But what was she going to do now? For the first time in her life she didn't seem able to make a logical choice. She was on her own with no support and she could not tell anyone what was happening. But that was most of the trouble, she didn't know what was happening and it was driving her insane.

One more squeeze of her brain and she felt that she, Colly – the rebel, the Republican, the business person, the mother and daughter – would be obliterated forever.

Sitting at the table with her head in her hands, she felt desperate. For two minutes she sat like that; then she was up and pacing the room again. This had been her behaviour for the past few hours.

Constantly she spoke to herself. She chastised herself about all the indoctrination she had been gullible enough to swallow. Then she contradicted herself, thinking she was right to have done what she did at the time.

Nothing else would have created a climate for justice we have, she thought. *We needed to do what we did to get to today.*

At other times she laughed to herself, "Wouldn't it come as a shock to people to know what I was doing with some of my time when I was supposed to be working?"

At other times she wrung her hands and cried.

"Why don't they ring? Dear God! Please let them ring," she repeated again and again.

The three men always rang as soon as they were home safe. It was second nature to them to touch base with her and they had never returned from any job without checking in. They wouldn't leave her like this thinking the worst. She just knew something must have gone wrong!

For some reason she had wanted to go with them this time. Something, which she couldn't put her finger on, had bothered her all along about this operation. The preparation beforehand had been meticulous, they had all done their homework and everything should have gone according to plan. But the feeling of foreboding prevailed.

Her mind was racing, trying to think back to what they could have missed or left to chance. They had done all the usual reconnaissance and had checked every inch of the area. Tom had walked the road around the whole area many times, and there wasn't a better operator.

He had a mind like a computer and logged every detail. He knew every movement on the road, who lived where and who shouldn't be in the area at any particular time. He knew every by-way and stick and stone, and spent many days and evenings getting used to the terrain. Firstly he had done it in daylight and then at night in the dark. He had left nothing to chance.

Nobody passed any remarks on him. People got used to him wandering around the countryside over the years. He loved the fresh air and nature as a whole. He collected wild animals that were injured, brought them home and looked after them. No one passed any remarks on him. He wasn't that fond of many people and didn't have much to say. Not many impressed Tom and most people thought of him as a bit odd.

As the older folk said, "He kept himself to himself."

Tom was introverted to a certain extent and a little taciturn. He also hadn't a great tolerance of what he called "numbskulls waffling". Chris claimed you got that with a lot of intelligent people.

Colly thought it was that he just never stopped calculating the odds of any given situation.

She laughed to herself, "If you stood near enough to him, you could probably hear the cogs of his brain whirring."

But he was thorough and that was all that mattered. He lived and breathed his chosen path and his dedication was unquestionable. His belief in his way being the right way was entrenched in granite. When he spoke, which wasn't too often, his companions, who had themselves all developed doubts lately, came away wondering if maybe Tom's way was after all the right way. They had all started out with very firm beliefs in their ways and their methods, but over the years this had changed.

Dear God, thought Colly. *After twenty odd years and no solution, you have to question if your way was the right way and the only way.*

Colly knew that she had been questioning herself and her three comrades' way of doing things very seriously for quite a while now.

A lot of sleepless nights had been spent by her lately going back over the past two decades. She was beginning to think that Tom was too much of a fanatic. He was intelligent and educated and now for some reason she expected some change in him. But he just continued on the same path with the same obsessions and never varied his thinking.

Surely he should be more analytical, she thought. *Question everything and realise that as time goes on and circumstances change, a person should re-evaluate the situation. Wasn't that the*

3

intelligent thing to do? What you thought was the right way to go twenty or twenty-five years ago may not be the right way now. Things have changed, she argued.

But Tom never questioned their methods. He believed he was right and there was no question about it. It was black or white, one side or the other, no grey areas.

Maybe, thought Colly, *he is afraid to change after all these years. Was he afraid of going back to being on his own? Maybe I should have talked to him more!*

She remembered one night when she broached the subject of their campaign with him and of trying to resolve the conflict through peaceful means rather than the gun or the bomb, and he had almost blown a fuse. She had to listen to him give her date, way and circumstance of how the Irish had been betrayed by the British and how you couldn't trust them, ever. It was the longest conversation she had ever had with him.

They had argued about it for hours. She had tried to put up a convincing counter-argument believing that they should look at where they had been, where they were now and where they should be going, but she just could not get through to him.

She also knew at that time that she had a lifetime of her own history to trawl though and analyse before she was totally convinced herself that he was wrong.

She knew the horror of what had happened in Northern Ireland since the end of the sixties and long before. She knew the arrogance of the British and their condescending attitude towards the Irish. She thought they still saw the Irish as the same potato farmers that they had starved to death or made to leave their own country over one hundred and fifty years before.

She also thought that a lot of the Irish politicians were what she could best describe as "West Brits" who kissed the English ass and would sell Ireland out to the highest bidder, be they English, German or other. They certainly would not stand against the British Parliament for the benefit of the people of Northern Ireland. She could not understand why they could not hold their heads high and stand up and say, "We are Irish and proud of it, this is our island, now get your asses out of it and back to your own country."

She knew it was all down to economics and she hated this. She looked at all the people were going through and saw the Irish and British politicians as corrupt.

She felt that if there were enough strong men in the Dáil, with a bit of backbone, the Troubles would have ended years ago and was often heard to say, "If Charlie Haughey had stuck to his guns and not backtracked, we wouldn't have to use ours now."

Colly went to make another cup of coffee, started to drink it, but put it down again.

"For God's sake," she snapped at herself, "you're hyper enough, you don't need any more caffeine. Come on! Get a grip on yourself. You've got to calm down, this isn't helping."

She looked at the telephone as if begging it to ring.

The last time a phone call was so late was when Tom and Pat had gone to move an arms dump when they were warned that someone had leaked its location. They were a bit wary of the information they had been given and were afraid it was a set-up.

Taking fishing rods, they had gone to the lake near the location and sat for hours, watching and fishing. After a while they realised that the information they had got was true and the place was being watched by the Special Branch. They sat on, fishing. The Gardaí and the Special Branch came and questioned them and looked for their fishing license, but Tom being Tom had everything in order. They even shared a cup of tea with them from the flasks.

Arriving back later at the car, they discovered it had a puncture and on the way home it developed another. This ended with them having to walk almost ten miles. Afterwards they had laughed about it, but with them being so late she had worried.

She chided herself now but she knew there was nothing she could do about it. The four of them had been together for so many years now, and in some ways they were closer to her than her own family. For one thing, they were the only ones who knew what she did in her 'spare time' and in fact held her life in their hands. One word from any of them and her life as she knew it would change forever. In fact, she would probably spend the rest of her life in prison.

Now she was worried and she knew she had good reason to. They were just too late for something not to have gone very wrong, over twenty-four hours too late.

A very bad feeling haunted her about tonight, she did not know why and she could not rid herself of it.

They got the information about this movement of arms by the Loyalists weeks before. They knew when, where and how. The source of the information was as sound as you could get, but nevertheless they had checked through another contact and the information had come back as very definite.

They knew that this cache of arms was very important for the UDA and was meant for something big on the southern side of the Border and had to be confiscated or destroyed. It could not be left in Loyalist hands to kill and maim Catholics.

The terrain they had to work in wasn't the most difficult in the world; they had been in worse, a lot worse. The whole operation had been worked out to the very last detail, or as Pat said, "To the last hundredth of an ounce of Semtex." The man was a genius with explosives and anything electrical or mechanical.

As someone once said, "Give him a box of matches, a fuse, a couple of wires – and he could blow up any place."

Colly got up from the chair and walked outside to try and relieve the tension. The evening was getting late and the last rays of sun were slowly ebbing over the horizon. She walked down towards the sea but for once she could not take in the beauty of the area she lived in. The wide expanse of Donegal Bay spread out in front of her. The frothy tides and its wondrous waves thundered along the sand towards the shoreline. This area was renowned for its coastline all over the world. Tourists and anglers came from America and Europe to fish or just to wander around the area. Americans especially loved the local town of Ballyshannon with its history and the fact that it was the oldest town in Ireland. People once left the port there for many places around the world, especially the US.

The four comrades were a rare bunch of people by any standards to even be friends, never mind to have carried out all the operations they had over the years and to have got away with it and never been suspected, which was amazing. It would have astounded the majority of people who thought they knew them.

The four were: Tom, the loner and a farm worker; Pat, who was not, as Colly once described him, "the Belfast Bimbo" but a very astute and respected solicitor; Chris, the seemingly happy-go-lucky engineer; and of course Colly herself, the level-headed, very attractive computer programmer and business advisor.

Colly started to think of all the others and how they had come into her life. Chris she had known since she was young and he was like a brother to her. Then there was Pat and Tom. Tom was a very rare choice for any of them to be associated with, but all of them had the greatest respect for him even if they did not always agree with his thinking.

They were a rare combination, and even rarer, soldiers of war.

When Colly thought of Tom, she looked on him as a man that loneliness had honed and shaped and knew she was very right about this.

He was born on a farm in Co. Clare on a late August evening. He was the eldest of three children – one girl and two boys. His parents were ordinary people – of medium height, medium weight, fairly attractive and hard-working. The only unusual thing about them was their deep love for each other. So deep and one-to-one that young Tom always felt left out. Tom remembered spending many long lonely days on his own on the farm with no one taking very much notice of him. He was ten when his brother came along and twelve when his sister was born. Much too late to be companions and too late to make any difference to his loneliness.

By that time the mould was set. Another thing that shaped Tom's mind was the fact that his father was determined that Tom would never end up working on the farm. He himself had never wanted to be a farmer. He resented the fact that through his own father's failing health and finally his death, he had to run the farm for his mother and sisters. In those days there wasn't much choice, but he was determined that Tom wouldn't end up the same.

The fact that Tom loved the life on the farm didn't come into it. That was the one thing they had in common – if they believed in something, then nothing or nobody would change their minds, no matter what the argument. His father thought if he educated Tom well enough, he would turn his back on the farm and do something better with his life. Having put him through college, he sent him to America when he graduated.

Tom reluctantly went but with only one aim, and that was to make enough money to put a down payment on the farm which he was determined to buy off his father. He knew that his father wanted to sell the farm and thought if he had enough money saved, then his father would realise how serious he was about working on it and would sell the farm to him. He spent a couple of years working two or three jobs and saving every penny. There had been no social life and only one aim – to get back home and buy the farm and make a home for himself on it.

At first, when he went to America, friends tried to get him to come out socialising with them but realised after a while he was not interested and that they were not going to change his mind.

He continued like this night and day, eating, dreaming and sleeping the farm. The next ten years were all worked out in his head. What he was going to plant, rear and breed. Where he was going to get the money to do this and even who he would have working for him. As he lay in bed at night he could see the farmhouse and how he had it painted. He could see the corn in the field and almost smell the cut hay. It was all he thought about.

Writing home regularly, he sent money to be put in the bank towards the cost of the farm. But only a few weeks before he was due home, he received a letter from his father that almost destroyed him. The news was devastating. The farm was sold. He couldn't believe it. In one letter his world had been destroyed. He just couldn't take it in. His father could not do this to him. He knew how much he wanted the farm.

"For God's sake that's why I'm in America, to make money to keep the farm. He knows this!" he roared, as he read the letter.

It was a major blow to him, so much so that he spent the next three weeks drunk. Those who knew him worried for his state of mind.

According to Tom it was touch-and-go whether he would stay in America or return to Ireland, but he was an Irish man who had to have Irish earth under his feet and so he found himself once again in Dublin Airport.

Mulling around the arrivals, he saw a stand with maps and bought one of Ireland. He had no idea where he was going to go. He bought a cup of coffee and looked at the map. He looked at Clare on it but he knew he had no home there to go to now that the farm was sold. He didn't want to see his father or mother. He felt they had betrayed him. As far as Tom was concerned, they should have understood his feelings about the farm and given him the chance to run it. If it hadn't worked out, then he could have sold it but Tom knew he would have made a go of it. He was so upset about losing it that it had never occurred to him to look for another place to buy and put the deposit he had saved on. Now any place in Ireland would do, and that's how he came to take the bus to Donegal. He had never been there and thought it was as good a place as any.

The next few months were spent just wandering the county, staying in different places and being very much a loner. He toured most of the county and finally he decided he had made the right choice. It was breathtakingly beautiful with some of the most spectacular scenery he had ever seen. He spent a lot of time along the shores or wandering around the little villages and towns. Or he would head into the mountains staying in country houses when he could, just to get a feel of the land again. He eventually started to work on farms. Anything to do with the land or animals and he was content. It wasn't his own land, but it was the next best thing. He didn't socialise a lot but spent his time reading and exploring the countryside.

Tom would have continued like this if something hadn't stirred his blood and got him thinking about the way he was living his life. The '81 hunger strike was the catalyst that changed everything for him and gave him a very different goal.

When it started, Tom could not believe that Bobby Sands would actually go through with it. Then Francis Hughes and Ray McCreesh died. After Bobby Sands died, Tom started to question his attitude towards the partitioning of Ireland. He started to read his Irish history again. He read *The Singing Flame* by Ernie O'Malley and he read it so many times it almost became his Bible. He couldn't believe that men could love their country so much and believe in a cause so deeply that they would lay down their lives for it. Then he thought of his farm and he knew just how they must have felt.

"This," he said, "is my country that they are dying for; what am *I* doing?"

From then on he began to plan. He knew he had to do his bit.

He started to go to pubs and dances. He got to know a few people with the reputation of having Republican tendencies and he would chat to them, but never offered opinions himself. He was biding his time; he had to weed out the "barstool mouth" from the "real thing". As he was trying to find someone to trust, he was not idle. He moved around, working everywhere and anywhere and keeping his ear to the ground, collecting as much information as he could.

Tom had one great advantage over other people – everyone trusted him. He didn't say too much and never talked about other people so he was told things they would never tell anyone else. He was accepted in places other people wouldn't have been allowed.

He worked for prominent men in businesses and farms. He was very competent and had a great business head. Many men would have been glad to keep him on in their employment, but when Tom got what he wanted he "upped sticks" and moved on to the next target of information. He was still not doing anything positive with his knowledge and he was getting frustrated.

One day when he was in a milking shed on the Donegal/Tyrone border belonging to a "staunch Orangeman", he overheard a conversation between the farmer's son and another young man. From what he could make out, there was to be a delivery of guns and explosives and they were debating where it should be delivered and where it should be stored. Tom heard the lot and it seemed like an omen to him. These guns were going to be used to kill Irish men and women and he couldn't let that happen. He spent the rest of the day worrying about what he had heard and finally he devised a plan. He would let the guns come in and he would watch where they hid them, and then he would wait for the right time and shift them and hide them somewhere else.

And that's what he did. He worked it all out. Another person would have used a van or a lorry and done it at night, but not Tom. He took a donkey and cart, which he felt would look more natural in that particular area. Nobody would pass any remarks on him drawing turf on the day the operation took place. That was what he was supposed to be doing anyway, drawing turf home, maybe not from that particular spot but "that was only incidental," Tom muttered.

The area that the guns had been stored in was on a bog bank belonging to the other young man. They had made a turf stack over the guns. Tom went in from the side, very gently pulled out the arms, stacked them in the cart, and covered them with turf. He restored the turf stack to almost exactly what it had looked like.

He then moved the guns about three miles to a cave in the hillside which he had found a few years before and had visited often. He liked the tranquillity where he would light a fire and boil some tea and watch the countryside from a vantage point. He knew that very few people knew of its existence and even less visited it.

Anyway, he thought, *they could be concealed so that no one would detect them, with a few rocks and lichen*. When he'd finished and looked at his handiwork, he was very pleased with it and said to himself, "That was a piece of cake. Now let's wait for the shit to hit the fan."

Everyday he carried on as usual. He went to work and waited to hear something. Day after day he waited but nothing new or out of the ordinary happened. He decided he would have to let the farmer know that he was thinking of leaving soon. It was expected that he would not stay around for much longer anyway. Tom was a loner and a wanderer, never stayed in one place nor had he any binding ties – that was the consensus of opinion by all. Tom would leave and that was that.

Two days after he had left the farm he heard on the grapevine that the farmer's son had finally discovered the arms were missing. No blame was put on Tom – it never occurred to anyone that he could be involved. Perhaps it was because he said so little and had no friends, and people assumed no one man would do this job on his own. Some even forgot he was around at all. It wasn't that he was impolite. If anything, he was the opposite. He had a very gentle way about him; he spoke when he was spoken to but never really initiated a conversation.

He still didn't know what he was going to do with the arms but he didn't care as long as they were not in the hands of the Loyalists.

Everything went on as normal for the next few months until one day when he was out walking through the woods near his work. It was early, around seven in the evening, and one of those times when you felt great to be alive. The fading sun still lent a gentle warmth to the air. You could smell the trees and the flowers, and the birds chirped in the bushes. Strolling along or "daundering" as he called it, he was listening to the ocean in the distance. Lost in thought and totally at peace with himself, he wandered on until suddenly he realised he was not alone.

He turned and glanced at the man who had stepped up beside him, and recognised him immediately. He didn't know his name but he had seen him in different places recently and had felt as if he had been watching him. He didn't really feel in any danger or that the stranger's motives were sinister. In a funny way he felt as though his destiny was finally going to be fulfilled. He had a definite premonition that his and this stranger's futures were going to be connected in some way.

Tom walked on at his ease and never said anything.

It must have been two minutes later when the other man spoke.

"I'm Chris Cassidy, you're Tom Hayes," he said.

"Am I now," said Tom, ever the man of few words.

"You don't say much, do you?" asked Chris.

"Only when I've something worth saying," said Tom.

"I've been watching you for a while," said Chris.

"I thought that," said Tom.

"Did you now, that's interesting. And why do you think I've been watching you?"

"Different folks, different strokes, who'll ever know what another man thinks?"

Chris was getting more and more curious about Tom, he couldn't quite gauge his humour. Did he know why he was there? If he did, it obviously didn't bother him – that or else he was one hell of a good actor. He decided to try another approach.

"We know you've got them, you know," said Chris.

"And who's "we?"" asked Tom, evading the obvious.

Chris decided to take a leaf out of Tom's book and proceeded with, "Their own didn't take them so we decided it must have been one of ours that did the job. But we came up empty-handed when we investigated that line. So by the process of elimination, you were the only one left."

"As I said before, who are "we?"" said Tom.

"Before I tell you who we are or are not, as the case may be, I want to ask you a few questions, OK?"

"We'll see," said Tom, being his usual cautious self.

"What did you intend doing with the guns and ammunition?" asked Chris.

"Hypothetically speaking, you mean," said Tom. "I still haven't said I have them."

He still wasn't sure who Chris was. He could be Special Branch, although he didn't think so. He knew all the Special Branch in the area.

But still, he thought, *they could have drafted in some new ones.*

He looked at Chris again. *Naw*, he thought, *he's not the type.*

"Hypothetically speaking then," said Chris.

"Maybe we can go about this another way that might bring both of us some answers. Firstly, I want to know what your politics are," said Tom.

"Republican," said Chris.

"Well! That's a start," returned Tom. "Are many of you working around here then?"

"A few," answered Chris.

"I need to talk to somebody," said Tom.

"Talk to me. I know you don't know me and you can't take me at face value but unless you do, nobody else will talk to you and we have a few questions we need answered."

Tom knew he needed to be able to trust someone and he felt this was his chance. Saying that, he was afraid he might be wrong and then what would happen? He would really be in trouble. If this man was

Special Branch, then he was a goner; if he was Loyalist, he was a goner. If he was anything other than IRA, he was in trouble.

Damn, thought Tom. *What do I do? I want to play to get involved and I don't want to wallow in confusion anymore, and I can't do anything on my own.*

Fuck it, he thought. *It's now or never.*

"Right," he said. "Here's what I want," and he started one of the longest conversations anyone had ever heard from him then or afterwards:

"I want to become an active member of the IRA and I want to fight for my country. For the last two years all I've worked for and thought about is how I would go about it. But I want to work with a unit that is tight, maybe two or three people. I want that unit to have only one man who would contact any other unit. I want each member of that unit to have equal say in any job that is being carried out. I want each member of the unit to be above suspicion and have very little contact or no contact with any other unit with the exception of the one 'go between' member. We decide on a job, our contact man informs the OC of the area and he sanctions or rejects it."

"Good God! You certainly have been thinking about it," said Chris.

"Yes, I have," returned Tom. "You may think that I am a very arrogant git dictating terms like this but I've watched what has been happening over the years and there is too much information getting out. The Special Branch or the RUC or the Army are sometimes on the spot even before the IRA even get there."

Chris sat on a fallen tree and looked at Tom with a smile.

"You've got quite a lot to say for yourself this evening for someone who usually hardly opens his mouth," he laughed. "I think there is someone you should meet. I'll meet you here same time Thursday evening. I may want you to come with me to meet someone then. While I'm here, can I ask you something? Why have you never got involved before now?"

"I've never met anyone I could trust," said Tom.

"How do you know you can trust me?" asked Chris.

"I don't know, but something tells me to and I'm fed up waiting. I want to do something positive to resolve this bloody situation and I want the Brits out. It's all I care about. I need to do something and I need to be with people who think like me," Tom replied.

"Right," said Chris. "See you Thursday evening then."

Tom watched Chris leave. He stood there for a long time afterwards. He was twenty-six years of age and he felt as though his life was only about to begin. He felt that everything that went before had been leading up to this moment. All before this had been about what someone else thought he should do – his father, his schoolteachers, his employer, or circumstances one way or another. Now he was going to do something that he wanted to do and he wanted to do it with his whole heart and soul. He also felt that he wasn't going to be alone anymore. This man who had just left understood him and they could work together towards their common goal. He felt a huge sense of exhilaration, something he could never remember feeling before.

If you had told Tom at that moment that he was being romantic and that his outlook was unrealistic, he would have laughed at you. He was going to fight for his country and what could be more realistic. The invaders of his country had to be got rid of and he wanted to do that.

Tom turned for home, deep in thought. He didn't know what tomorrow or any of his tomorrows would bring, but now he eagerly awaited them.

The next evening Chris took Tom to meet Colly and Pat, and that was the beginning of one of the strangest relationships, that developed between the four of them. It took them through many dangerous situations and many decades.

Chapter Two

When Chris introduced him to Colly and Pat for the first time, Tom felt instinctively that it was the beginning of a relationship that would last his lifetime.

Colly remembered well how Chris had come to her on the night he first spoke to Tom. She was at home and the children were all in bed. The topic of the disappearance of the arms dump had, over the months, taken up many hours of conversation between them. It wasn't usually something that they would have heard about or even have expected to hear about, except for the fact that it was in a small rural area and the people who had hid it were a couple of amateurs and were so shocked at its disappearance they had forgotten to be discreet.

They found it very funny but Chris was determined to find out who had done the job and what they were going to do with the arms. That and the fact that he wanted to shake their hand. It had taken him quite a while to work it all out but he was now left with only one conclusion which he was sure was the right one. The others had their doubts about it.

When he said he was going to confront the man he thought had done the job, they were a bit wary about it. But Chris had a good instinct and had been watching Tom for some time and seemed quite confident about his theory. He had done a lot of research into this guy so they decided to trust his judgement and let him get on with it.

Their unit would meet in Colly's house at that time, sometimes staggering their times of arrival. One would come to the back door and one to the front. It was quite easy to cross the fields or park up the road and walk down to her house. Lots of people walked that area, especially on the beach. Nobody passed any remarks. Her house was inconspicuous, lost among the trees and it was easy to jump the wall and disappear into them. Also, once you were inside the front gate, you could not be seen from the road. If you drove around the back of the house your car was hidden and if you jumped the back wall which the men often did, the trees covered you.

Colly was into conservation in her own small way and hated high walls and concrete jungles, and she surrounded the house with all forms of trees and shrubs, some of which had been there since her grandmother's time.

Sometimes they wondered what people thought of their relationship and decided they only saw them as friends. It couldn't be completely hidden in a rural area but Chris and Colly had gone to school together and had always been friends. Pat was seen as a friend of Chris's.

Chris would laugh and say that you could get lost in Colly's half-acre if you didn't know your way around it. There were huge oak and beech trees along the perimeter dotted around with lilac and other scented flowering trees thrown in for good measure. The house was about one hundred and fifty years old. It was two storeys high with ivy growing up the walls. It included four bedrooms, a sitting room, two bathrooms and a great kitchen.

Everyone loved Colly's kitchen. To look at it, you would think it had been there forever but it was only ten years old. At least that was when it had been renovated. When the house had been left to her by her grandmother, what was now the kitchen had been a kitchen, pantry and dining room in one. Now it was one large room. The top half contained a great Aga cooker, the working and cooking area and a scrubbed wooden table that everyone sat around. The lower end was the sitting area dominated by Nan's big chair.

Colly often smiled when she thought back on that time and would look to heaven and blow a kiss to her saying, "Thanks, Nan."

Colly was on her own at that time, separated for six years and rearing her children, having left her husband who now lived with another woman in England. The fact that her marriage was over was only a relief to her. It had been a mistake from the start and she knew she should never have married him. At only nineteen years of age and pregnant, she had been stupid enough to marry a man she didn't even know. But she had learned the hard way.

She considered herself a fairly intelligent woman and often wondered how she could have been so awfully stupid to marry the man she had married. But then she knew that many other women could sing the same song. She was not alone. The two of them had nothing in common and as she had often thought, *I knew absolutely nothing about him yet I was planning to spend my life with him.*

She said to herself, "I ended up knowing him all right though!"

She knew his violence, his bad habits, his lack of intelligence, his lack of hygiene and his total disregard for his children. She'd had four in the four and a half years they had been married. Colly loved her children and they loved her, and her ex-husband did not come into the equation. They were now her kids and only hers. He didn't come to visit them and didn't even send a birthday or Christmas card. She just hoped this did not make a difference to the children. But she knew they were better off without the violence disturbing them everyday.

At the time her grandmother died she had been in dire straits. She had no money and was trying to work, study and rear her children.

She loved her Nan and only for her she might have thrown in the towel long ago where college was concerned, but she had kept her going. She spent as much time as she could with her, helped her with her college work, read her assignments and babysat often for her. They talked about everything under the sun and after that, what was out there in the galaxy. Nan was that kind of person, interested in everything. If you didn't intend to tell her something, she got it out of you anyway. Colly never thought of her as old and she had certainly never thought of her as dying.

From a very early age she'd realised that her Nan was a lot more interesting than anyone else she knew. They would sit together in a big armchair in the kitchen in the evenings when Colly was small, and her Nan would tell her stories about her life when she was young.

She told her about her father, Colly's great-grandfather, who was an old IRA man. Of how she sometimes wouldn't see him for months because he would be away in other parts of the country fighting for "Ireland's freedom". Of how he would come home, and she and her mother would go to a 'safe' house just to see him for a few hours. Or of the nights she would lie in her bed and hear the door opening, and she would hear her father's voice. Later he would sneak into her room and she would hug him and they would talk for a while. She would fall asleep in his arms and when she would wake in the morning, she would not know if it had been a dream or reality.

She told her of the Easter Rising when wild rumours had been raging through the country and no one really knew the truth of what was happening, and how they had waited to see if he was one of the dead or whether he was even in Dublin. It was a few days before they received the news that he was on his way home.

As Colly listened to her Nan's stories she felt as though she was the little girl waiting for her beloved father's return, and she could feel how her Nan had felt.

As she grew older, her Nan's stories went on to her relationship with her father when she was in her teens. How he eventually came home and how he would tell her about his life on the run from the "British invaders". Of the people he had met and what they were like. Of some of the great men who died in the Easter Rising and their love for their country. Of the day they determined that Ireland would be free of British rule even if they had to give their lives for that to happen.

These stories had a big impact on Colly.

In the summer, Colly and her Nan would go for long walks. They wandered along the coast through fields of cows and wildflowers. They walked the shores and picked shells and seaweed, and they would make carrageen moss or dry some of it to eat. They roamed by streams and rivers and walked through woods. Nan was a mine of information and taught Colly about the birds and flowers and spoke of old wives' cures her grandmother used to make. Sometimes Colly really wanted to be back there when life seemed so much simpler than today.

When she was young she always held her Nan's hand and as they grew older, they always linked. When she thought of it many years later, it was like the child needed support early on from the older woman, and later the old lady needed support from the child. But it didn't seem like that at the time to Colly. She knew she could always rely on her Nan.

As she thought back on those walks, what she remembered most was the laughter and the songs and the stories. She could still see them standing on a beach or a road, bent with laughter, not fit to move and tears running down their faces at something daft one of them had said. Moving on, Nan would point out scenery or old houses and tell Colly the stories about them and about the people who lived in them or the legends attached to them. On those country roads, her Nan would often softly sing Irish songs which told the history of Ireland going back hundreds of years or teach her funny songs that she learned as a young woman and they would both sing together, at the top of their voices.

Their love for the sea was boundless and many days were spent wandering the shores around the area. Some of the beaches stretched for miles and were great to walk. On a day when the tourists had all gone home and all you could hear was the sound of the surf and the birds, you could not ask for anywhere more wonderful. Neither of them took this pleasure or the area they lived in for granted. They walked Rossnowlagh's wide expanse of beach for hours and the rocks at Creevy at all times of the year, in summer when it was crowded with holidaymakers or in autumn with the changing weather and the breeze calling for huddling up in hats and scarves and winter with the foaming tide and the wind blowing the cobwebs away.

Sometimes they wandered down the Kildoney roads smelling the hawthorn, wild garlic and daffodils while listening to the birds and feeling the sun on their faces. At other times they carefully stepped down the rocks to the shore at the Barhouse and sat on two of the big rocks dangling their feet in the water staring out to sea, at peace with each other's company.

Nan told Colly, "The sea is in your blood. When you are used to living beside it and you leave, you will always feel there is something missing. It's the sound and the smell of the sea and the pull of the tide stirring your blood and calling you back."

When her Nan died, Colly was in Belfast doing her final exams for her degree in Business and Computers. She had spent the previous two years studying through the Open University. She'd been going to college three days a week that year studying and her parents were looking after the children who were now aged from ten to fifteen.

She had loved her classes and working on computers. They were the way of the future and she was good with them. The scope of information she had access to and how she could find out almost anything at the touch of a button fascinated her. She was still amazed at how easy she found it to operate something that a few years previously had been a total mystery to her.

When the rest of the students had left college in the evening, she could still be found doing research, especially on solutions to problems she had come across during the day.

It made her feel that she was doing something positive with her life after all the negativity of her marriage breaking up and the feeling that she wasn't qualified for anything. It had been tough going but she had now reached the end of her studying. When she had walked out of the college that afternoon, she was one of the happiest women alive.

That was until her phone rang after she got back to her lodgings.

She didn't know how she got home. When she got the news about her Nan all thoughts of college were forgotten about. She just wanted to get home but found it hard to think logically.

There must be some mistake, she kept thinking. *She'll be there when I get home, waiting as usual.*

Halfway home on the bus, she wanted to get off. She didn't want to arrive home and find her worst fears confirmed.

She moved through the next few days and the funeral in a daze. Her darling Nan was gone and she wouldn't be there for her anymore. They said she just died in her sleep and she didn't suffer. It was a massive heart attack. To Colly it didn't matter what it was – Nan was gone and how she went didn't seem to matter.

"We didn't even get to say goodbye," she cried.

In the weeks that followed, Colly was inconsolable. Everyone was worried about her and no one seemed to know what to do with her. The children kept trying to console her but nothing seemed to work. Then there came a call from her grandmother's solicitor.

"Could you please come in to see me as soon as possible?" he asked. "I have your grandmother's Last Will and Testament here."

Colly hadn't thought about what her Nan may have left behind. All she thought about was the huge vacuum that she had left in her own life, and all she felt that would assuage her grief would be to have her Nan back, and she knew this was impossible. It felt as though she

21

was working on automatic. Sometimes she would forget that her grandmother was dead and she would feel alright for a while. Then it would all come flooding back very clearly to her what had happened and she would be devastated.

Her family were really worried about her. Until then, Colly had been the very strong one who had been able to deal with anything life had thrown at her. Now she was like a zombie one minute, walking around as though in a trance, and weeping uncontrollably the next minute. She didn't sleep at night and this really bothered her as she didn't want to think. She wanted to switch off her brain. She didn't want to remember. Nothing and no one mattered to her. She had lost the one person who had truly loved her and whom she loved as much in return. The one person that she could rely on to be there for her, who she could tell anything to, the person who taught her about life and gave her the courage to do everything she did and the one who understood how she was feeling without ever being told.

She loved her children but that was a maternal and a natural loving, but with her Nan it was different. She liked and loved her Nan because of the person she was and because of the way she lived her life and her amazing knowledge and generosity of spirit.

She couldn't foresee her life without her. When the word had arrived from the solicitors' asking Colly to arrange an appointment at her earliest convenience, all Colly thought about was that her Nan had left a message for her. That was all she wanted. She knew her Nan wouldn't leave without saying goodbye even if Colly couldn't say goodbye to her. So she rang the solicitors' and made an appointment for the next day.

At eleven o'clock the following morning, she arrived at the office where she was asked to take a seat and was eventually led into the solicitor's inner room. He proceeded to inform her that he had her grandmother's Last Will and Testament and that he would read it to her. Colly was actually surprised at the word "will". She had never thought of her grandmother having much to leave. She realised there was the house but she'd assumed that would go to her mother. She thought her mother should have been here with her too and wondered why she hadn't been asked. At first when the solicitor started to read, it all sounded like legal jargon to Colly. She let it all wash over her until suddenly she realised what the man was saying.

Her grandmother had left all her possessions to her. The house which she loved, £280,000 in a bank account, stocks and shares and all her jewellery. Everything she owned, which came to quite a sizeable amount.

Colly was in shock. She'd never thought of her grandmother as wealthy. She knew she'd lived comfortably and had never wanted for anything. She'd always bought her presents for her birthday and Christmas and they were always good, but never extravagant. Money had never mattered where Nan was concerned. She was just her Nan. Now Colly had just discovered that she had made her a very wealthy young woman. Even in death she was looking after her.

She would have given it all back if only she could have seen her Nan for one last time and said goodbye to her properly, but this she knew could never be.

As the solicitor was finishing reading the will, he told her there was one last thing. There was an envelope and there was a stipulation attached to it. It was not to be opened until she was in her grandmother's kitchen sitting in what her grandmother had described as "their" chair. He said that her grandmother said that she would know what she meant.

She looked at the envelope and knew that she now had all she really wanted from this man. Taking it from his hand, she thanked him, left the office and drove straight to her grandmother's house.

When Colly looked back on that day she felt as though she'd been looking down on herself. She remembered stopping the car outside her grandmother's gate, walking up the path, reaching up to open the door with her own key that she'd always had and pushing it open. She felt dazed. She remembered walking down the hall with its grey tiles with their muted design and homemade wool rugs. She remembered noticing the strong banister running up the stairs and thinking, *I've always liked that staircase*. She also remembered holding on to the envelope in her hand and feeling as though it weighed a ton, and then pushing the kitchen door open, feeling anxious yet eager. On eventually entering the kitchen her eyes went directly to her grandmother's big armchair. Slowly moving towards it, she felt her heart was breaking. She wondered why her Nan had insisted on her reading her letter in this chair. Didn't she know it would break her heart?

Colly thought, *Well, it's the last thing that she has asked me to do and it's probably the last thing I will do for her.*

Easing herself into the chair, she sat for a while to get her bearings. When she'd left the solicitors' office, all she'd wanted to do was to read her grandmother's letter. The thought of how it would upset her to be in the house by herself hadn't occurred to her. It felt so empty and so cold even though the hot July sun was beaming through the big windows.

After a couple of minutes she opened the envelope and she read:

"My Darling Colly,

I am sitting here thinking of you and knowing that when you read this letter, I will no longer be with you, physically anyway, and that you will be a little upset.

I remember the first time I saw you – you were about three hours old. Your dad had come over to collect me and bring me to see you and your mum. When I got to the hospital you were in a little cot beside your mother's bed and I was amazed when I saw you. You had this head of auburn curls and you opened your eyes of blue and frowned, stared at me for a few seconds as though you knew me and went back to sleep. I turned immediately to your parents and said, "Isn't she a real Irish colleen!" and they both laughed and said, "Now there's a name for her – Colleen!" and that's what they called you. Of course when you became four years of age you thought it was too "prissy and sissy" and demanded to be called Colly from then on. You were a real tomboy. I always thought you were like me in that way. I hated the restrictions of being a woman. When the men were out fighting I wanted to be with them. Instead all I could do was join Cumann na mBan and all I got to do was run errands and type letters.

Sometimes I feel that I never really did fit into this life. When I was young I wanted to be a mechanic and later when I married your grandfather and had children, I wanted to work outside the home but it was frowned upon. Later in the civil rights era all I could do was organise meetings because people told me I had grown too old to do anything else.

You remember those meetings, I brought you everywhere with me. You always surprised me with your ideas and your grasp of things. It was then that I realised that you had grown up. It was also then that I realised that you could probably do a lot more in your life than I ever could.

That is what I want to say to you – I am not afraid to die. In fact, in a way, I am looking forward to it. I wonder what I will be the next time around. Maybe I'll be sent back as a man and I'll be able to do what I want.

You, my darling, have to go on with your life and do what you can. Love your family and friends, find your dream and follow it. Remember that I loved you above all in my life and I tried to teach you all I knew to give you knowledge and strength to decide what you wanted to do. You will be finished your exams soon and I know you will do well because you have a great brain. Maybe you could start your own business with the money I left you.

Oh! One more thing. I want you to build that dream kitchen that we talked about for so long and never got around to. I want to think of you in it but keep our chair and then you will know I'll always be there. I'll keep an eye on you from up above if they'll let me.

Goodbye my darling, please don't grieve too long, I would hate that. Get out there and grab life with both hands. Always remember I love you.

Your loving Nan."

Colly just sat there holding the letter. All of a sudden she felt as though the room had warmed up. She could feel her Nan's presence all around her. While reading the letter she felt as though she could hear her voice, soothing her and making her strong, knowing that what she had said was true because she had heard her say the same thing many times over the years. She knew there were many things she could do now which she would not have been able to do if her Nan had not made her a very prosperous young woman with her own home and money. But she also thought that no matter how educated or gifted you were there were things that a man could do, but were unacceptable for a woman to do, no matter how well they could handle it.

The money would now give her freedom to do a lot of things she wanted to do without being reliant on or answerable to others. She and the children were set up for life no matter what came up and that alone gave her a huge sense of freedom.

All her life Colly had a healthy disregard for male/female boundaries. When other girls played with dolls she was out with the boys playing football, wandering fields or cycling in the country. When she became fifteen, one of her friends tried to kiss her and she smacked him in the mouth. She didn't want that kind of carry-on; it would ruin her fun with the boys.

One of the disadvantages Colly felt she had was her looks. She felt she was too prissy and feminine looking. She was five feet five inches tall, slim, with a good figure and long auburn hair that cascaded in curls down her back. The blue eyes that she'd been born with had turned green with flecks of brown, she had a well-shaped full mouth and a pretty nose flecked with freckles. In her early teens she had hated how she looked. No matter how she dressed she always seemed to look girlie. Colly's uniform then was a pair of her brother's boots and trousers, an old jacket of his and a woolly hat with her hair tucked under it. No matter what her father or mother said, that was what she put on as soon as she came in from school.

First the homework was done and then she went out with the boys. She could be found fishing, catching tadpoles, sliding on frozen ice in the winter or jumping streams and climbing ditches, and there were always five or six boys with her and she invariably seemed to be the only girl.

She was accepted in her own right because she wasn't a "softy" like the other girls. She never cried when she got a scratch, she just got on with whatever she was doing. Some of the boys were a lot softer than her, in fact. Many times one or another of them ran home after falling or scratching themselves on a bush for Mammy to look after them. Not Colly; she just fell and got up again. This may have had something to do with her Nan's attitude; if it wasn't fatal, you'd get over it if you forgot about it.

She was also a very good student and this was something that surprised everyone who knew her. She loved school. She had a very curious mind which searched for information.

She was the same with everything in life. From studying nature to finding out how machines worked. When she was seventeen she bought herself a motorbike with money she had saved from doing summer jobs because she knew her parents wouldn't allow her to get one if they knew what she was up to. She taught herself to fix it when anything went wrong with it. Her parents worried about her riding it but her grandmother said that she was OK and well able to look after herself and the bike.

Nothing was the easy way out for Colly; as far as she was concerned it wasn't worth doing if it was. While other young girls were sunbathing on the beach she was abseiling down a rock face, canoeing or climbing mountains.

When she was seventeen she began to attend civil rights meetings with her Nan and she became very interested in what was happening in Northern Ireland and to her it was as though she had found her niche – fighting injustice. What made it even more important to her was that it was injustice of the British to the Irish people – her people. All her life she had heard of the oppression of the Irish by the English invaders and now she could see how she could do her bit to change things and get Ireland back to where it belonged – an independent country.

She and her Nan had found something they really believed in and became involved in, which gave them a purpose in life. They attended civil rights marches all over the country and believed that this was the beginning of the Irish people demanding to be heard. They were saying "no more" to the injustices and cruelty that had been meted out to them. They wanted one man, one vote; a right to jobs in Northern Ireland and the same rights as any human being; the right to decent housing in decent areas and a cease to harassment when a Catholic man went onto a building site in another area of his country to the point where his life was threatened or even taken. They also expected equal rights in education for Catholics and equal opportunities for jobs once educated.

Chapter Three

It was while she attended one of these meetings that she met her husband. Some friends of his had persuaded him to attend. She saw him during the meeting looking at her as though he knew her. Afterwards he had a friend of hers introduce him to her. He said they had met before but he couldn't remember where.

Colly laughed and said, "Now that's not a very original line!" and went to leave.

"Have you got a motorbike?" he asked.

"Yes! I have," she said.

"You were in Omagh a few Saturdays ago with two other people on bikes," he said.

"How do you know?" Colly asked.

"I was in the bike shop when you came in," he replied.

That was the beginning of the most disastrous relationship she ever had.

His name was Kieran Foyle. He was a mechanic with a half share in a garage. He and Colly started to talk bikes and he offered to take a look at hers. She arranged to meet him two evenings later at her house.

He was a very attractive looking man. Six feet tall, well-built, dark brown hair and brown eyes. He seemed very quiet.

They met nearly every second evening after that first meeting and she really enjoyed working with him on the bikes. Afterwards they would go to the pub for a few drinks with the lads. She found herself becoming really attracted to him and looking forward to the next time they'd meet. When she was with him it was like he was a magnet. She wanted to put her hands on him and feel his skin. He had a great body, well-toned and muscled. As time went on and Kieran didn't make a move, Colly decided she would have to or they would get nowhere.

When he arrived that evening, she was in the garage. She put on the kettle and made tea before they started work.

He sat on an old broken chair and Colly looked at him. He was talking but she wasn't listening. She walked towards him and put her fingers on his lips.

She heard him say, "Colly, what are you doing?" as she bent to kiss him.

Then it was like all hell had broken loose. They were devouring each other. It was as though they had been restraining themselves for so long and once that first step was taken, they couldn't get enough of each other. There was no thought of anything but each other. They just had to fulfil the need inside them. If someone had walked into the garage, they wouldn't have noticed. T-shirts and jeans were ripped off and they made love on the work bench. All Colly could hear was, "I've wanted you for so long, I've wanted you for so long," and it drove her wild.

Afterwards as they lay there completely spent, Colly started to laugh, "It's just as well Mum and Dad are away or they would have thought a hurricane had hit the garage!" There were tools everywhere, where they'd thrown them from the work bench.

That evening set a precedent for evenings to come. Only afterwards, they found other places to make love.

About five weeks later, Colly found out she was pregnant. She couldn't believe it.

OK, she thought. *We took no precautions the first time but every time since we have been very careful.*

But once was enough.

When Colly told Kieran his automatic response was, "Right! We'll get married."

She didn't know what to do. She really didn't know if she loved him. She only knew him six months in all and she thought that what she felt for him might only be sexual attraction. They really hadn't done that much talking. Their main conversations were about bikes. She got her intellectual stimulation from the people in the civil rights movement and sometimes it was a relief to be with someone who didn't argue the pros and cons of everything. Kieran had only gone to the one meeting. Whenever another one came up and Colly asked him to come, he always had something else to do.

She was in a dilemma. She wouldn't have an abortion, it was against her principles and she didn't want to upset her parents. She had to talk to someone.

Her grandmother was her only choice.

When she thought back on the conversation with her grandmother, she could only remember it going something like this:

"Do you think you could stick him for fifty years? Are you worried about living with the stigma of being an unmarried mother? Do you think your child needs him as a father? If you answer "no" to any of these questions, don't marry him."

For once Colly just didn't know what to do. Kieran was all for getting married. He would look after her, he said. Eventually it seemed easier to go along with his way of thinking.

They got married in a little church outside Donegal town. On the morning of the wedding Colly still didn't know if she was doing the right thing but she went ahead with it anyway. This was something she often thought about afterwards. If she had been true to her gut feeling they would never have married.

They moved into a flat in Kieran's hometown and everything seemed to be fine for the first few months. She sold her bike and bought a small car so she could travel back and forward to her father's hardware shop where she worked in the office. In actual fact they saw very little of each other. They were working during the day and Kieran spent a lot of evenings in the garage working overtime.

When the baby was born, Colly had to give up work and look after her, a beautiful auburn-haired girl called Saoirse. She loved her daughter from the first moment she set eyes on her and she couldn't believe Kieran didn't feel the same way. Instead he seemed to ignore her and started to drink very heavily in the evenings. Talking to him proved useless; he didn't want to know. Two months later, she realised she was pregnant again. When she told Kieran, he slammed out the door and she didn't see him until three o'clock the next morning. Waking when he came in, she asked him where he'd been and he became very aggressive and abusive. Realising he was drunk, she went to make him coffee. As she handed it to him, he swiped the cup out of her hand and hit her across the face. As she fell, he kicked her and left her lying there. In the morning her eye was closed and discoloured. When he saw it he apologised and pleaded with her to forgive him and promised never to do it again. But the scene was set.

He began to drink more and became more aggressive. Colly didn't know what to do. Then she discovered she was expecting twins. They were born ten months after Saoirse, and she named them Ruairí and Diarmuid. She picked the names herself as Kieran didn't seem to care what they were called. It was an effort for him to visit her in hospital. Only that his sisters insisted that he go, Colly didn't think she would have seen him at all. She thought he would be proud to be the father of twin boys but it didn't seem to matter to him.

When she came out of hospital, he started to stay out all night. If she asked him where he was going, he created rows and would beat her up. If she didn't, he would say she didn't care and beat her anyway. In the next two years she left him twice and came home, but each time he came after her and promised he would change and that he really loved her and couldn't live without her. But each time things got bad again after a few weeks.

Eventually, after they had been married four and a half years, she left for good. This time when she left, she had a couple of her biker friends warn him he was not to go near her or her children. A few weeks later she discovered she was pregnant with her fourth child. She had suspected it but hoped it was just stress that was causing her lack of periods. When she told her parents and grandmother, all they were worried about was that she would think of going back to Kieran but that period of Colly's life was over as far as she was concerned.

Like all wife beaters, Kieran was a coward and once he thought her friends would deal with him, he left her alone. When Róisín, her last child, was four, Colly decided she had to get her life together. She had to do something positive so she went back to work in her father's office. She spent a lot of time getting it together and bringing it in line with the modern 20th century, as she told him. She got him to buy a computer which she learned to use. They were amazed at how much easier it made everything. That was when she decided she wanted to do an advanced Computers and Communications course and maybe start her own business.

She went back to school and did the Open University course, and then on to college in Belfast where she finished top of her class. She was a wizard with computers.

During this time the one person that kept Colly going was her grandmother. She was her mentor and her psychiatrist. When she decided on anything, she would talk it over with her. Apart from the ordinary mundane running of life, they also discussed politics. When she got married, Colly had practically lost touch with the outside world and only knew from the television news or papers what was going on. Her grandmother had kept going to meetings and marches up until Bloody Sunday. Both of them in their own way would never forget that day.

She hadn't gone to Derry that day because one of the twins was sick and she'd been looking after him. In the evening, the phone rang and when she answered it, Chris was on the other end. He'd been a friend of Colly's for years and had been one of the people in the civil rights movement in their area with them, since the start. He was in tears; at first she couldn't understand him. He kept saying, "Did you see the news? Oh! Colly, did you see it, it was terrible, they just mowed them down!"

She put on the TV while she was talking to him and she couldn't believe what she saw and heard. Troops had opened fire with live ammunition on the people marching and killed – no one knew at that moment how many – at a peaceful civil rights march in Derry.

It was inconceivable to her that this could happen. For God's sake Ireland was a civilised country and no matter how arrogant England were, they could not mow down innocent people like that. But they did, and the proof was on the television for all to see.

Chris told her that he had been at the march and luckily for him, the crowd he had been with had gathered towards the back. They heard the shots being fired and for an instant it was as if everything stood still. Then pandemonium broke out. He couldn't understand what was happening. People started to run everywhere. They were screaming and crying and falling all over the place trying to get away. He eventually made out what people were saying.

"They are shooting at us, the British soldiers are shooting at us," they were shouting.

Someone grabbed him and told him to run, and in the mayhem he lost the people he came with. He did not know if they were alive or dead. He was now on his way to the hospital to see if he could find them. He said he would ring later to see if she could get in touch with anyone.

When Chris got off the phone, Colly rang her Nan. She hadn't heard anything about it. She'd been in bed sick all day and hadn't turned on the TV or radio. Colly packed the children into the car and drove to her grandmother's. When she arrived, some of the crowd had returned from Derry but some were still missing. Everyone was in a terrible state. They were completely stunned and shocked at what had happened. They spent the evening phoning around trying to find out if everyone they knew had got home safely, and eventually all were accounted for.

As they talked into the night, the feeling was that this was the start of something dreadful. Once again the British had treated the Irish as nothing but animals without rights to be shot down if they dared object to the oppression they were living under. Something had to be done. Would the Irish government stand for this? They now had to do something to stop this total disregard for human life. When Colly returned home that night, Kieran had not come home and didn't arrive until the next morning. When she tried to talk to him about what had happened in Derry, he didn't want to know. He couldn't understand why she was so upset and told her to shut up about it.

"No one belonging to you has been killed so what are you carrying on about?" he said.

Those were the words that finally made Colly decide to leave him. She couldn't live with someone who had no principles and no ethics, who couldn't understand how heartbreaking it was to see one's own countrymen shot down in cold blood like animals, someone who wanted to do nothing about it and couldn't care less.

She knew that things were really bad between her and Kieran, with the beatings and his total lack of interest in the children. But somewhere deep inside she had hoped he might change. Now she realised that there was nothing in his makeup to help him change. Not even compassion for another human being. He was a totally selfish person and nothing or no one was going to change that.

Colly decided that she was going to leave him and she started to put into action how she would do this. She knew that even though he didn't love her he would not let her go easily.

She put on the greatest show of her life for the next few months. She agreed with everything he said and bent over backwards to keep him from suspecting her motives. When she had it all worked out, she put it into action. She waited until he had gone to work one day and she packed all her own and her children's belongings and she moved back in with her parents.

Later that day, three of her friends paid a visit to her husband and told him in no uncertain terms what would happen if he tried to contact her. Like all bullies, he was easily cowed.

After Colly moved back in with her parents, she continued to attend civil rights meetings. The attitude to the North was changing. A lot of people who were involved in the movement were leaving. They were afraid to march anymore in case they would be shot. The rest of the attitudes were becoming hardened and angry.

It was obvious that the Jack Lynch government was going to do nothing. There might have been some hope if either Neil Blaney or Charlie Haughey had been made leader of the Fianna Fáil party at that time, but to most people, Jack Lynch seemed not to have cared less.

They should move him to the Falls for a few years and maybe he would change his mind.

But, thought Colly, *Jack Lynch didn't have the backbone. He was an economist and if it wasn't viable economically then he didn't want to know. It would have cost Ireland a lot of money if the country was united, and to hell with what was happening to her people.*

Patriotism didn't come into it or concern for his own people as far as Colly could see. Every day there were more and more reports of harassment and assaults coming from the six counties. It was bad enough that they had put Catholics in ghettos but now they were directing their Unionist marches through these areas, and it seemed, with the blessing of the RUC and the British Army.

Chapter Four

It was around this time that Colly and Chris started to spend more and more time together. They had been friends since school and now found that they were thinking along the same lines as far as the Troubles were concerned. Uppermost in their thoughts was the idea that they had to do something to help but they had not yet quite decided what. They spent hours trying to work out what would be the best direction to take.

Looking back at this time, Colly thought all she seemed to do was work, look after her children, discuss the Troubles and look for a solution. They were meeting two or three nights a week and finally the consensus of opinion seemed to be that there was only one avenue of action to the problem and that was to "bomb the Brits out of Ireland."

It was war and the British had declared it, and all British military personnel and politicians were legitimate targets. That's when the first problems loomed – they needed arms and ammunition and they were ignorant as to where these could be acquired. With the determination and anger pushing Colly and Chris, this to them was a trivial matter to be solved whatever way possible.

Chris knew a few men in Northern Ireland who were of like mind and he said he would talk to them. Colly's grandmother suggested that they would contact the old IRA that were in the area and see what they would suggest. They also decided that if the only way that they could help was by locating supplies of ammunition, then that was what they would do, and would make sure they would get it to where it was needed.

One very funny thing happened around that time after they had spoken to some old IRA men, one of whom lived out in the middle of the country and said he would "do a bit of visiting" and see what he could come up with. About a fortnight later, he arrived at Nan's door in an old pick-up truck, entered, sat down and had a cup of tea. Nan noticed he had a big canvas bag with him and when he was leaving, he handed it to her and said, "Can you see that these get to the right people?" He then left.

When Nan looked in the bag, there were six guns of various makes and ages. She nearly had a heart attack. She didn't know how the gathering of arms was going to be organised, but she didn't expect them to be handed to her in a shopping bag after a cup of tea.

After he rang Chris, he got in touch with someone he knew who was running an IRA unit in Tyrone. Chris was told to leave them in a certain house in Lifford. He was given a password to use so there would be no mistakes. He did this and heard nothing further for about a month.

One evening some time later, the phone rang and his contact asked if he would meet him. Chris had known this man for years and at one time they had worked together in Dublin. He trusted him – he came from a strong Republican background and many nights they had discussed many ways and means of fighting the atrocities taking place in Northern Ireland.

Having met him and after the usual small talk, he asked Chris if he would be willing to take guns and ammunition from Mayo to the North. He said they had been there for a few weeks and he wanted someone who wouldn't be associated with the IRA to do the job. These guns were urgently needed. Chris agreed to do this and he was told that contact would be made with him in the next few days with the details.

When they parted, Chris worried about telling Colly and her Nan about this or if he should carry on by himself. He finally decided to tell Colly but not her Nan. He felt he needed someone he could trust to know where he was and what he was doing in case he got caught. He just didn't bargain for Colly's reaction. He thought later that he should have known better how she would react. She had never yet, as far as he knew, been afraid of anything and she was determined to do her bit in the fight against the British. She insisted she was going with him.

Her reasoning, as far as she was concerned, was logical. If the two of them went to Mayo and stayed overnight, no one would think anything of it. They would look like any other couple going away for a night to have time on their own. They could book into a bed and breakfast, collect the arms the next day, tour around for a while and come home. The next day they could be delivered to Lifford. Chris knew from past experience that there was no arguing with her.

About a week later, they set off for Mayo, driving to Westport and stopping in a little pub where they had a drink. They then drove around the town and came across a little lodging house on the outskirts and booked in for the night. After a nice leisurely meal, they went on to another pub where they spent a few hours. They had made arrangements as to where they would collect the guns the next morning. The meeting place was to be at a side road just outside the town. This was all done with a very laid-back attitude, or at least it looked like that from the outside.

When it was all accomplished and they were on their way home, both Chris and Colly started to laugh. It started off as an ordinary fit of the giggles but developed into something that was verging on hysterics. Chris had to stop the car because he couldn't continue to drive until he controlled himself. They then both realised that they had practically been holding their breath in case they would be caught.

When they finally controlled themselves, they continued the journey and were relieved to get home safely. Next day, the guns were delivered to their destination by Chris who encountered no problems. In the next year to eighteen months, this was repeated a few times. The collection places and destinations changed and the cars and vans they used were different, but they never had any trouble. After the first time the fear was never as great, but they never took any unnecessary chances.

Colly's Nan was never informed by them of their activities but they felt she knew. When they were away for a night, she knew they'd gone but she never asked where or when they would be back. Colly's mother looked after the children.

Chapter Five

After a couple of years and a few jobs shifting arms here and there, Colly decided she should go back to learning. She and Chris discussed it over a period of time and both decided the best solution would be for Chris to continue doing what he could, and she would go back to school for a few years. She had the idea that if she could get her own business going, she would be free to do what she wanted to do. Once she was her own boss she wouldn't have to answer to anyone if she was a few hours late, or why she was going to a particular place when another place might provide better business. She also wouldn't get tied up in lies. She was tired of arguing with her father about what was best for his business and his lack of adventure in expanding. She had her own ideas of what she wanted to do in that area as well.

Even though she'd got him to open a second shop in another town and to agree to hire a manager to run it, she knew this was as far as he was going to go. It wasn't enough for her. She wanted to go as far as she could with her life, in all areas. She hated playing it safe.

Anyway, her heart was set on starting her own business and it wasn't running a hardware shop for the rest of her life that she wanted. She knew quite a lot about running a business from working in her father's shop but she needed more training and she was determined to get it. Over the next few years, she spent her time studying and trying to get an educational foundation which would help her achieve what she wanted with her life. It was time to get her life together.

She also felt she had to take a step back from the Troubles and decided to look at things for a while as her emotions were getting in the way of her thinking. She had to think of her children and the danger she was putting herself in. If anything happened to her they would be without a parent who cared about them. Their father hadn't been in touch with them since she'd left him, so he couldn't be relied on to look after them. Her parents had reared their own children and she couldn't expect them to rear hers. She needed to rear them, and when they were older she could do what she wanted.

There was an ambition in her now that she never remembered feeling before. She often thought that if she were to say where it came from, she would pinpoint it to the realisation she had when herself and Chris began to move the arms that in the future, anything she put her mind to, she could do. Now she was going to work out what she wanted to do with her life and she was going to go for it.

Mentally, at this time, she felt like two people, as though she had a split personality. On the one hand, she just wanted to get her home together and rear her children. She loved them dearly and couldn't foresee her life without them. She wanted to give them everything she could and to make life as good as she could for them. She also wanted to work for herself and to make something of her own life and to be able to say she'd achieved something such as her own business and made it a success. She didn't want to have to rely on anyone anymore.

All her life she seemed to look to others to help her solve her problems. It was either her father who gave her a job, her grandmother who she went to when anything was wrong in her life, or even her husband, who she thought was the solution to the problem when she got pregnant. Now she wanted to stand on her own two feet and work out what she wanted to do in her life by herself.

It wasn't that simple. Even though she knew what she wanted for her children and for her working life, she had a belief that seemed to be embedded deep in her soul that she was passing the buck if she didn't stand up to be counted and do her bit for her country and justice in the North of Ireland.

Each day, in the papers and on the television, she saw more injustices being perpetrated. She had friends in Strabane, Derry and Belfast who wrote to her and rang her, telling her of more and more acts of cruelty and oppression being committed by the British Army and the RUC.

She started an Open University course and then went on to college and graduated with honours. A few months after graduating, she started her own business as a Business and IT advisor and within a year she was making a very healthy salary. She had businesses all over the country which she worked with. She not only supplied information on the practical and financial sides, but she set up IT system networks to suit individual companies. After another twelve months, she had three others working for her and was going from strength to strength.

Chapter Six

From time to time, she visited friends in Belfast and would often end up in houses listening to catalogues of complaints from women whose children were being harassed and beaten by the British Army.

On one occasion she went to visit Laura, a friend of hers in Ardoyne, arriving on Thursday evening for a long weekend. They talked long into the night and Laura told her how worried she was about her son. Ben was thirteen. She felt he was more and more inclined to lean towards the Provos and she was getting very scared for him.

Her husband was already in Long Kesh. He had been lifted one evening as they were having tea and locked up. Laura said the only thing he was guilty of was trying to help young fellows in the youth club stay out of the IRA. Eighteen months later he was still inside without trial or without having committed a crime. What she was really worried about was that at least three or four times a week, Ben was being stopped and searched by British soldiers, either going to or coming from school.

He had arrived home on a few evenings with his jacket and shirt torn where they had really got rough and thrown him about between them. Ben was getting angrier and Laura was afraid he was going to do something crazy. She had taken to walking to school behind him every morning. On two occasions, while she'd been there, the Brits had stopped and questioned him but hadn't touched him.

Laura realised that while she was around, Ben was safe from beatings or harassment but she knew she couldn't follow him every morning. She had her own work to go to. Also he was embarrassed with having Mammy walk him to school. She didn't know what she was going to do.

As they talked, Colly and Laura decided that Colly would follow him the next morning and see what happened. At 8.30 she let Ben out the door before her and then she left about a minute later, following about 200 yards behind. Ben had just turned the corner when Colly heard the sound of an army jeep screeching to a halt.

As she rounded the corner, she saw Ben being pushed up against a wall and his jacket being pulled off him and thrown on the ground. His school bag was emptied out on the wet street but worst of all was the language of the soldiers. They were calling Ben a "Fenian bastard", shouting that his father was a murdering animal and what they were doing with him in Long Kesh and that they would soon have him grassing on his fucking Provo friends. They also told Ben that he was jail fodder and a thick Paddy and it was a waste of time him going to school as he was too thick to learn.

Colly walked slowly up to the scene, all the while taking in what was happening. She felt really scared, not of the soldiers, but when she looked at Ben's face. He was standing, looking at the soldiers and the look of hatred on his face was dreadful. His eyes looked so cold you could almost see him plotting revenge. She felt a shiver go down her spine. Bending down, she picked up Ben's coat and put it on his shoulders. One of the soldiers told her to "fuck off you Fenian whore." She ignored him and continued to pick up the schoolbooks and put them in the schoolbag. She felt cold as stone. These soldiers were just scum and were to be treated as such.

She put Ben's bag on her shoulder and put her arm around his shoulder, and started to walk away with him. All the time the soldiers were making smart comments but neither Ben nor Colly passed any remarks.

When they had gone about five feet, one soldier grabbed Colly's arm. She looked down at his hand on her arm and then into his eyes. He dropped her arm as though it had burned him. Colly then turned to the rest and said, "Do you know that you are the best recruitment officers the IRA have?"

She then turned and walked on. No soldier said a word and she knew she wasn't just thinking of Ben being recruited. Neither of them spoke as they walked to the school. When they reached the school, Colly said, "We'll talk tonight, Ben."

He said, "Fine" and went into the school.

As she looked after him, she thought, *No thirteen-year-old should look so worried or be treated like that by anybody.*

He looked as though he had all the cares of the world on his shoulders.

"This is just not right. This harassment of the children has to stop somehow before it's too late for boys like Ben," she said to herself.

Laura had told her already that Ben's schoolwork was suffering and he was becoming more and more remote from her. Up until then, she and Ben had been very close but now he was clamming up when she tried to talk to him and he was getting more and more angry. Colly could see the future for Ben. He would stop working at school and eventually drop out. He would, in the not too distant future, be one of the boys in balaclavas with guns or bombs and unless he was really lucky, he would one day be brought home in a coffin. Something had to be done, and soon, to stop this from happening.

Colly was twenty-seven years old, had been married and had children, but Ben was just starting life. Unless things changed, his life might be very short and he wouldn't get the chance to do any of the normal things that ordinary young men look forward to doing.

As Colly walked back to Laura's house, she tried to think of what could be done to change the situation. There had to be some way of dealing with it. The soldiers had the power to do – and they did – anything they liked, but surely the people had to have some power too. They had to get together to stop this from continuing.

When Colly talked to Laura, she asked her if there was any way people could get together and write to their elected representative and kick up a racket to stop this abuse of their children. Maybe they should think of policing their children going to and coming from school. Laura said there were various groups who were looking at all these problems and nothing seemed to be happening. She would make a few phone calls and see if she could get the people together for a meeting.

The next night, fifty people turned up along with a Sinn Féin and SDLP representative. If there had been more time, a lot more would have attended. The meeting was informal with a lot of anger and shouting. As expected, a lot of different attitudes were aired, from the totally despondent to "Let's blow the Brits out of the North."

It went on late into the night. The mothers seemed to be the ones with the strongest opinions and none held back in delivering them. They were all very worried about their families. Eventually, it was decided to set up a rota of parents escorting their children to school for the time being. Meanwhile all the pressure they could think of, through pen and voice, was to be put on the authorities to stop this harassment.

Some of the more politically minded men and women were going to talk to various politicians to try and stop the children being harassed.

As Colly left the meeting, one of the men approached her. He laughed and said, "Well! What is a wee Donegal woman doing sticking her nose into Belfast politics?"

Colly smiled and said, "Oh! It's one of my failings. I can't keep my nose out of anything."

He laughed and said, "So I hear."

She looked at him. "Do I know you?" she asked.

He laughed. "Not yet but I have a feeling that will change. I'm going to Donegal in a few weeks time; I'll call to see you."

"I don't entertain strange men," Colly said. "You obviously know me but I don't have the same advantage."

"Sorry," he said. "Let me introduce myself. I'm Patrick O'Hagan, originally from Donegal, but I've lived in Belfast for the past fifteen years."

"Pleased to meet you," she said. "I'm Colly…"

"I know who you are. We have a mutual friend, Chris Cassidy."

"Really, do you know Chris? We've been friends from childhood."

"Yes! I know," he said. "Chris and I went to school together and then on to college. He told me you were here and to keep an eye on you in case you got into trouble. Do you often get into trouble?" he asked.

"Not unless I can't help it!" she replied. "Have you seen him lately?"

"Yes, we're in touch quite a bit. And we run into each other every now and then. He keeps me up to date with all you and him get up to," he grinned.

Then the penny dropped. "Ah! You're his friend Pat that he is always speaking about. And I doubt if he speaks about all we get up to."

He smiled and said, "Oh! You'd be surprised what I know! We must get together for a drink when I get to Donegal. Tell Chris I'll be in touch. See you soon."

As he left, Colly didn't know what to think. He was the type of man she usually steered clear of. Tall, dark-haired, tanned, a smooth talker, a snappy dresser and not to be trusted as far as you could throw him. Thinking this, she realised that Chris trusted him and that he was a very good judge of character. But no, she was not having a drink or anything else to do with this fashion plate. To Colly he spelt trouble – she didn't know why, but she did know that she was staying well away from him.

She left Belfast the next day and went back to work. Life returned to normal – work, looking after the kids and running the house – her days were full.

But she couldn't forget what had happened in Belfast. She thought about Ben and Laura trying to make a life for themselves and coming up against impossible odds. From Laura's husband being interned and her struggle to rear Ben on her own to Ben losing his father whom he loved and having to put up with all the harassment from the British. The odds really were stacked against them. Colly felt more and more angry.

Just because the British soldiers had guns and it was legal for them to carry them, they thought they could do what they liked. They went into houses and tore them apart on the smallest pretext. They tore up furniture and dug up the floors, and the only reason there seemed to be for this was if a father or son had been interned. Often there was only the mother in the house with the children. When they couldn't get what they wanted from the parents, they went after the vulnerable little children.

They had to be stopped.

On one of the weekends that Chris called, he and Colly decided to take the kids for something to eat. The usual pizzas, hamburgers and chips – most kids' favourite food – was bought and duly washed down with a few quarts of fizzy drink. Afterwards, they all spent a couple of hours trekking through the countryside. As they watched the children running on in front of them, Colly started to reminisce about her grandmother and her life as a young person, and it reminded her of Laura and her problems. She found herself talking to Chris about all that had happened in Belfast. He told her that Pat had been talking to Laura, and had rung and said that he was coming down the following week.

Colly had met him a few times briefly since she had seen him in Belfast but hadn't really got to know him. Chris told her he was involved in something hush-hush and he wasn't talking about it. She thought, *Yeah! He's probably admiring himself in the mirror.*

But Colly was disturbed. She didn't want to see this man again. She couldn't explain it. She just felt very wary of him and started to question Chris about him. How well did he know him? How did he know he could trust him? She told him she thought Pat looked like "the male version of a Belfast bimbo" and looked as though he spent hours preening himself and selecting his wardrobe.

Chris laughed uproariously.

"You have this man very wrong, Colly," he said, "but you'll find out yourself in time what and who he is. By the way, I'm going on a training session next weekend. I've asked if you can go and I've been told to bring you along."

Colly couldn't believe her ears. She'd always wanted to go on one of the IRA training sessions but hadn't been allowed. She'd heard from Chris what they involved. They were like survival weekends, and involved unarmed combat; how to use a gun; the dismantling and putting together of guns and generally surviving in rough terrain.

Chris had taught her a lot himself, knowing how interested she was in any physical exercise and that she was a pretty good hand at using a rifle. Colly didn't know how she would deal with anything else though. Both of them had spent quite a few weekends trekking through mountains, climbing rock faces, fording rivers and sleeping rough. She had loved it. Anything that pushed her body almost past endurance gave her great satisfaction. She was always setting herself goals and pushing herself to meet them. This weekend would be an ambition fulfilled, especially as it was mostly men who trained on these weekends, so she knew she would be up against it.

At the back of her mind, she also knew that if she went on this weekend there would be no turning back. One way or another, she was committing herself. Everything would change – she didn't know how, but she believed it.

They continued speaking of many things until Colly said, "I have this idea where three or four individuals could set up a unit and work undercover, away from everyone except for one or two people in the

IRA. If this could happen and there was a leak, then we would know where the leak came from as there would be only five or six people involved altogether. The jobs would be decided, set up and carried out by these individuals after discussions and agreements. No one else would be informed except that one contact within the IRA hierarchy."

Chris said, "You've certainly been thinking. Are you sure you want to get involved again? You do know that if you go on this training trip and get involved in missions, there will be no going back."

"I know I have to get involved," she said. "I can't just walk away and expect everyone else to fight for what I want. This is my children's future and the children in the North's future. It is my country and I have to do what I can to bring justice to the North."

Since she'd left Belfast, she couldn't forget the brutality of the soldiers and the contempt they had treated her and Ben with. They were foreigners in her country and they had the bloody cheek to talk to her like that.

Nobody does that to me or mine, she thought.

She felt that these foreigners were walking the streets of her country terrorising and browbeating her fellow countrymen, and nobody seemed to be able to stop them.

The next week was spent making arrangements for the children to be looked after for the two days Colly would be away with Chris, and on Friday evening they met and headed off. He wouldn't tell her where they were going. He just said he would tell her when they were there.

It was early morning as they left Donegal and eventually entered Leitrim. They spent their time travelling up and down mountain roads. Colly had a feeling she was being taken in circles and wherever they would end up, if she ever went looking for it again she would never find it.

After a while, Chris stopped the car and handed Colly a balaclava and a black jacket. She already had a pair of black combat trousers and a black polo neck jumper on. He told her the balaclava had to be put on and was not to be taken off while she was in camp. She pulled it on over her head and put the jacket on. It was a bit big but it would be warm. She also had a pair of black leather gloves. She rolled up the sleeves and pulled on the gloves. By this time the balaclava was stifling.

"Christ, I'll never stick this for twenty-four hours," she said.

"Don't worry about it," he said. "After a while you'll get used to it and you won't even know you're wearing it. If it was one of the old wool ones, you would be driven mad with an itch but these ones are made of synthetic material and are not so bad. You can take it off for the moment because now we walk and it wouldn't do if you were to meet anyone wearing one of those. I'll tell you later when to put it on."

They headed off at a good pace, up lanes and over fields and ditches for about two or three miles.

Colly said to Chris, "What about the car; won't someone think it curious it being parked there all of this time?"

"Don't worry about it," Chris replied. "Someone will move it and leave it back on Sunday morning for us. All is taken care of."

After a while, Chris said, "Stick your balaclava on."

She did as she was told and as they came out of a clump of bushes, she found they were in a clearing at the bottom of a rock-strewn hill. They stood and looked around.

Colly said, "Is this it?"

Chris said, "Yes. Shush, quiet for a few minutes."

He stood and listened.

"OK," he said. "Come with me."

They circled the clearing and about halfway around it, they went into the bushes and out the other side, where to Colly's surprise she saw an old cottage with its windows boarded up. There seemed to be nobody around. Then Chris started to whistle. After a few seconds a figure appeared from behind the cottage.

Colly was amazed. He walked over to them and greeted Chris and Colly in a low voice, and they all walked into the cottage together. He was dressed in the same fashion they were and Colly could make out no distinguishing features. No part of his body was showing except for his eyes.

There were about ten other people there, all dressed alike, talking in low voices. In the corner there were two men standing together at a table. Chris walked over to them. One of them looked Colly's way and nodded and turned away again. The other man turned, stood with his hands behind his back and said in a Derry accent, "We're splitting the camp up into two units. I will take one of them and my comrade here will take the other. As I put my hand on your shoulder, I will say left or right and you will move to the left hand side of the room or the right."

As he separated those present, Colly realised she was not in the same group as Chris but she didn't have much time to think about it. The next thing she knew, she was being ordered out of the room, with the rest of the unit, by their commander.

For the next few hours she was crawling on her belly through gorse bushes, climbing the hills she had seen earlier and trying not to break her neck on the shingle. All the time she could hear this Northern Ireland voice shouting, "Get your fucking head down or do you want it blown off," or "Move your bloody arse, have you got lead in it!"

At one point she was bending down trying to cross a stream when the commander came up behind her and pushed her, shouting, "Move, move!"

She ended up face down in the water.

She felt like turning around and smacking him one on the jaw but she realised that was what he wanted. Just because she was a woman he expected her to crack.

They are not going to break me, she thought. *I'll show them.*

This went on well into the afternoon. At about four o'clock, they were back in the camp and were given soup and sandwiches. The evening session was taken up with map reading. At around eleven o'clock they were told that they could sleep for a few hours.

Colly looked around for the beds and quickly realised that they were supposed to sleep where they were on the floor. She saw a pile of old newspapers in the corner and took some of them. She put one of them under herself and the others over her. Her commander looked over, nodded and said, "Good thinking, comrade."

Next thing she knew, she was being rudely awakened.

"Up! Up! You're not here to lie around all morning. We have work to do."

Colly groaned – she felt as though she had only just fallen asleep. It was still dark outside. When she looked at her watch, she saw it was only 6.05am.

As she looked around, she was shocked and thought, *Jesus Christ! They have moved in an arsenal.*

There were guns of all sizes and descriptions on the tables against the wall.

Bloody Hell, she thought. *I hope no one has tipped off the Gardaí or we'll have a full scale war on our hands.*

"Right!" said the same voice from the previous day. "I'm going to show you how to dismantle, clean and put together various guns. Remember; learn well, as one day it may mean the difference between life and death, and that life may be yours."

For the next three or four hours, Colly was completely engrossed in trying to do as she was told. She found it all fascinating. She cleaned and put back together all the guns she was given many times, each time quicker than the last. She became very proficient at it. She was also getting familiar with the feel of the smaller gun in her hands. There were still very strong doubts in her mind about whether she would be able to kill another human being – British or not – no matter what the circumstances. She doubted she even could.

They broke for lunch at about noon. Soup and sandwiches again. Afterwards her unit was taken out into the clearing between the hills for drill. The same bloody-minded commander from the previous evening was in charge and he was doing nothing to stop her hackles from rising.

This shouldn't be too hard, thought Colly. *Left, right, left, right – anyone can do that.*

They had all been given rifles and lined up. Then orders were shouted at them. Colly didn't mind this. Chris had shown her the drill before and she had watched quite a few colour parties train at her grandmothers' over the years. But nobody else seemed to know their left from their right. When she turned right, as directed, the guy beside her would turn left and walk into her, going the wrong way.

Chaos reigned for about half an hour with everyone trying to get the formation right. All the time the commander was roaring, "Are you all fucking stupid? Do you not know your left from your right?"

If he didn't shout so bloody much, thought Colly, *he might get better results.*

After a few hours, when they finally seemed to be getting it together, they were told to follow their commander at double quick time.

He brought them through a pathway in the trees to another clearing. There were targets set up on the other side of it in a row like great big dartboards. The commander ordered them to lie on their stomachs until he could see what kind of shots they were.

With her first shot, Colly nearly broke her shoulder. She hadn't realised how strong a recoil a high powered rifle had.

The next thing she heard at her ear was the commander shouting, "You bloody stupid woman, I suppose you've broken your shoulder now!"

"No, I'm alright," she said, through gritted teeth.

"Now let me show you how to do it properly," he roared. "Listen, watch and learn."

Gradually she was getting better, she wouldn't win any competitions but she hit the target nearly every time. Her shoulder was hurting a lot but she was not going to give in to it. She couldn't let that bloody-minded ass know that it hurt.

Later, as they marched back to camp, she felt quite pleased with herself. Her shoulder still hurt like hell but she had survived the exercise and did as good as most of the men and better than some.

When they arrived at the cottage she could smell the stew and she realised she was starving. She hadn't seen Chris since just after they'd arrived and she wondered if he would be there. He wasn't.

After dinner, they had a talk on incendiary devices and explosives. They were shown trip switches, mercury switches and were told how they worked, along with other explosive materials and devices. Colly was really interested, and as usual, was more than willing to learn. She asked questions all the time about the difference between dynamite and Semtex, and the explosive effects of each of them. All of this was discussed, books looked at and diagrams shown. They talked long into the night.

Finally their commander said it was time to sleep. In the morning, he said, they would leave at staggered times starting at 6.00am and every half hour after that.

Colly lay down on her papers and wondered where Chris was but she didn't wonder for long. As she closed her eyes she saw the commander look at her and she thought, *You bloody hard bastard*, and she fell asleep.

Chris woke her in the morning. "Come on," he said. "We're leaving, some have left already."

She looked at her watch – it was 7.30. She couldn't believe she had slept right through the first departures.

"Are you ready?" said Chris.

"Lead on," she said.

As she was going out the door, her commander was coming in. As she passed him, he said, in a soft Belfast accent, "Not bad for a wee Donegal woman."

She nearly choked. She stood still and looked at him. He winked and chuckled and walked on.

She couldn't wait to get out of the cottage.

When she came out, Chris was doubled up laughing. She was raging with him. "You knew all the time. Why didn't you tell me?" she shouted at him.

"Oh! I would love to see your face," he said. "It's a pity it's covered with the balaclava."

Colly had recognised that soft voice. It was Pat O'Hagan, whom she had thought of as "that Belfast male bimbo" in Ardoyne. She couldn't believe it. There was no sign of the male bimbo in the man who shouted orders and abused the troops for the past few days. He certainly had not acted like any fashion plate during the previous twenty-four hours. He was like two different men – one of whom could have graced the pages of a magazine, and the other the tough man with very little finesse.

Chris was still laughing and she could have thumped him.

"Why didn't you tell me!" she seethed at him.

"Oh! We thought you should find out for yourself," he laughed.

"What do you mean?" she said. "Did you tell him what I thought of him?"

"Oh yes," said Chris. "He found it very funny. I'm sure he is roaring his head off now with laughter after your reaction."

"He's like a chameleon," Colly said thoughtfully. "Like two different people."

"Yes," said Chris, "that's how he works. He can fit in anywhere. I told him of your idea of a secret unit in Donegal of three or four people with only one contact in Northern Ireland. That's why he was so anxious to see you on the training session and how you'd react. He wanted to see what you were made of and whether you would break. You passed with flying colours. He says you are a tough nut to crack and not afraid of taking orders, and let me assure you that was one hell of a tough session. I don't think I've seen a tougher one; he really put you through it."

"What do you mean? Did you see the training I did?" asked Colly.

"Yeah! Some of us were monitoring it from the hill. We like to see how our protégés are working out," answered Chris.

"Now what happens?" Colly asked.

"We have a few things in the pipeline that you, me and Pat must discuss. You have to make the decision about how involved you want to be in all of this. He will call us within the next fortnight and we will work things out. He thinks you are like him – you would fit in anywhere and could go anywhere without anyone suspecting you."

Chris pulled off his balaclava and told her to do the same. She then realised that he had been right – after the first few hours, she'd forgotten she had been wearing it.

When they arrived home, Colly realised that she had indeed a lot to think about. She didn't know what Pat O'Hagan expected from her or indeed what she was capable of delivering. She could use a handgun, but saying that, she didn't know if she was capable of using it to shoot someone. She also knew that she was capable of blowing every military and Unionist building out of Northern Ireland but she didn't want innocent victims hurt. She also knew that she wanted to shoot the soldiers in Belfast who had given Ben such a hard time and she wondered if she ever came up against them again, would she be able to do it? She knew she would never forgive them but was that hatred carried to the rest of the Loyalist community in the six counties? All of these things would have to be thought out.

She decided to wait and see what Chris and Pat O'Hagan would come up with and then she would make up her mind. One thing she did know was that she did not want to sit idly back and do nothing, but as to what depth of commitment she wanted to make she still wasn't sure. It was one thing to talk of strategies but another to carry them out. Was she willing to put her life on the line? Was she willing to risk her family life for it by being imprisoned if she was caught?

At the moment all she knew was that she wanted to see Ireland free from those thugs that roamed the streets of Northern Ireland and get all the Brits back to England where they belonged. Yes! She had a lot to think about.

Chapter Seven

Pat O'Hagan was born in Letterkenny on a beautiful summer morning. When his mother first laid eyes on him, the sun was beaming through the window as she looked at him in her arms. She always said that it continued to shine on him as he grew older.

He became the apple of her eye – he was an only son with two sisters. When he came into the world, his father was still studying at university in Dublin to be a research scientist. He was a highly intelligent man, sort of absent-minded and quiet. He and Pat's mum had been childhood sweethearts and from the moment that she set eyes on him, she decided she would marry him.

What Mrs. O'Hagan wanted, Mrs. O'Hagan got.

They had been married a year when Pat was born. She was from a very well-off family and she had a large inheritance from her grandparents, so money was no problem for them.

When Pat looked back on his earlier life, he could not remember his father being very prominent in it. He always remembered his mother and sisters being there, but the only recollection of his father was of a vague figure drifting in and out at the weekends making very little impact.

He wasn't an uncaring man and it was obvious that he loved Pat's mother very much. He just didn't seem to be able to communicate with children. As he walked past Pat or his sisters, he would touch their heads or look at them as though he was surprised that they were there and amazed that he had produced these little human beings. As far as the practical needs of his children were concerned, he was lost.

"If he could have kept us in a laboratory and treated us as specimens he would have probably had more interest in us," Pat mused to his mother at times in his teens.

When he was in his twenties, Pat asked his father about his attitude towards his children, and he said he was amazed at what he and Pat's mother had produced. He was fascinated by how his children grew and learned, and the similarities he could see in them, their mum and himself.

"Maybe," he said, "I was too much the scientist and not enough the father."

Pat laughed and told him, "Maybe you still are!"

As the kids grew up, their father would buy tickets for football matches, shows or Christmas pantomimes in Dublin and take the children to see them, but they all knew that he would rather be back in his laboratory. Eventually it was Mum who took the kids everywhere. There was no resentment felt towards their father. They knew he loved them in his own way, he was just different. Pat's mum was great fun to be with and she didn't mind joining in the fun. They went on holiday without Pat's father once, and it was such a success they continued to do so.

As Pat grew older, he began to understand his father more. He realised that seventy-five percent of his mind was given to his work, twenty percent to his wife and five to the rest of the world. He couldn't be any different and Pat accepted him for what he was.

School for Pat was easy – he enjoyed the academic side of it and was also very into sport. He was the type of person who didn't have to work very hard at anything to be very good and he was very popular with everyone.

As he entered his teens, his father was offered a new job in Belfast and he and Pat's mother decided that they would move the whole family there.

At first Pat found it very hard to settle in a big city school. He felt as though he had to prove himself before he was accepted. The first couple of weeks were very hard. One of the things he found hardest was that it was a mixed school and he had never been taught alongside girls before.

He needn't have worried. With his looks and wit, he became very popular with them and once they discovered he could pass himself at sport, he won the boys over too.

It was at this time that he met Chris; both of them having been born in Donegal gave them a common bond. As time went on, they found they had a lot more in common. They became best friends and went almost everywhere together. They joined clubs, learned the guitar and dated girls. Chris was more introverted than Pat but they seemed to balance each other out. Pat with his confidence, good looks and natural wit and charm was invited everywhere, and where Pat went so too Chris went.

Pat was also a born leader and he had very definite ideas about things. He wasn't exactly dogmatic but if he made up his mind about something it would take a lot of proof and a good argument to make him change it. Many a man tried it but very few succeeded and many ended up siding with him. Possibly that's why he and Chris got along together so well – they thought alike. Neither could tolerate injustice to either dog or man and neither had a problem with speaking out against it. It is probably why both found themselves literally fighting it a few years later.

When the civil rights action groups started in Northern Ireland, both of them joined and went on the marches. Although both came from fairly privileged backgrounds and knew that when they finished their secondary education they would probably move to Dublin or back to Donegal, it didn't mean that they couldn't do their bit and protest against the injustices they could see around them in Northern Ireland while they were there – especially those perpetrated on the Catholics in Belfast at that time and down through the years of history.

At first, Pat didn't do too much real thinking about the problems that the civil rights campaigners were protesting against; he was just walking the walk and talking the talk, but without much depth of thought.

"Oh! Yeah! One man, one vote is every man's right, and Catholics should get a better deal. I will be out there protesting with them. Lead on, my man, I'm with you," was his attitude.

But after a few meetings, he found himself being co-opted to committees here and there.

It was "still no big deal", but gradually he found his attitude changing and hardening. Each day he had to listen to grievances about discrimination against Catholic workers from people in every other aspect of life. There was harassment of Catholics on building sites; abuse of Catholics who wanted to work in different areas; Catholics being turned down for jobs because they were just that – Catholics; Catholics being burned out of their houses because they had the "cheek" to actually buy a house in a Protestant area; Catholic teens being beaten up because they strayed into Protestant areas.

Belfast was like the pogroms in Poland in the last World War where all the Jews were put in ghettos and not allowed to live anywhere else. A Catholic couldn't better him- or herself in Belfast or Northern Ireland at that time because the whole system was against them. If you wanted to do better, you had to emigrate.

Pat was seventeen at this time and at a very impressionable age. By the time he finished school there, he had worked for two years in some of the most deprived places in Belfast. He had a huge insight into the people and the deprivation there. This experience was to contribute to how the rest of his life would be marked out.

He and Chris had applied to University College Dublin. Pat was to study Law and Chris Engineering, and both were accepted. They could have stayed in Belfast and gone to college there but both decided that they wanted to get away for a while. They felt as though they were under a lot of pressure being involved in the civil rights and other groups and that their education would suffer if they stayed. Both had been brought up with the belief that they had to qualify in a given profession to have the power to change anything. Pressure from both families had a lot to do with their deciding on Dublin to finish their education.

Like most boys in their late teens, there was also the idea that "far off fields were greener."

They believed that a different social scene and another city would be more exciting. There was also the feeling they wanted to go home; the two young men always saw the Republic as being their true home and couldn't get used to the North being seen as British. Donegal was home but Dublin would do for the present.

Whether that thought was conscious or unconscious, it was definitely true in Pat's case. Even though he had not lived in Donegal for a long time and the family house there had been sold, it was still where his heart was and going to Dublin, he thought, was the first step in going back there. He intended, when he qualified, that he would practice in the Republic – if not in Donegal itself, then somewhere in the Republic.

Like all young people deciding what to study at third-level and where, it was a major decision and at that age, one has very idealistic views. Pat thought long and hard about his decision and the deciding factor was that a good lawyer was a major need for the civil rights movement. Especially if that lawyer had, like him, been in at the grassroots and knew the discrimination that was happening in Northern Ireland. He thought he could change the world like a lot of young people, and do much better than the older generation had done before him up until then.

He looked at the older generation and arrogantly thought that they had made an awful mess of things. Often, this may have been the case but, as in the majority of cases, a young person's idealism will soon be knocked out of them by life and just trying to survive as best they can.

When Pat went to Dublin filled with ideals and enthusiasm, he intended to do what he could to promote the civil rights campaign from there and to make the people in the Republic take notice of what was happening in Northern Ireland. He wanted pressure put on Stormont by the Dáil to change their policies. He wanted more protest marches and debates and he wanted the people to rise up and be counted.

He started to study anything he could relevant to the civil rights law. He wrote to papers and to whatever head of state he thought could help to influence England. He studied Martin Luther King, Che Guevara and information about any other civil rights leader he could get his hands on.

Most evenings he was at a meeting or a debate or a march. At the weekends, he went back to Belfast to report what was happening in Dublin and to find out what was happening in Belfast. Sometimes he would only spend a few hours in Belfast and then go on somewhere else to a march or meeting. He ate on the run and studied on the run and always seemed to be cramming more and more into his life. After a while, he found he could do with just about three or four hours of sleep at night.

Pat was lucky when it came to studying. He had a very retentive memory and he never wasted time. He wouldn't drive anywhere; he would take a train or bus or get someone else to drive him. As far as he was concerned, the time going from one place to another could be spent studying or writing. He was never short of someone to drive him. Women galore lined up for the job.

One of the most amazing things about Pat was that he never realised how attractive he was to women. He had a wacky sense of humour and also a very serious side to him. He was what might be described as one of the "new men".

He accepted that women should be in whatever walk of life they choose to be in – politics, law, cleaning the streets or staying at home looking after the family. He would have as good an argument with a woman as he would with a man and they loved him for it. If someone told Pat that a certain woman drove him to Belfast because she fancied him, he would say, "Don't be ridiculous, she wanted to go to the march," and he would believe it.

That doesn't mean he didn't date girls. He did, but they were few and far between. It wasn't one of his priorities.

That was until he met Jilly. She was Pat's female equivalent in mind and the exact opposite in looks. Whereas he was "tall, dark and handsome", she was small, about five feet two inches tall, blonde and outgoing. But in the one way that really mattered, they were the same – they both hated bigotry and discrimination of any kind.

They met at a meeting which was advertised under the heading of 'Equal Rights for Everyone' at the college. Pat was one of the speakers and so was Jilly. He spoke of the civil rights movement in the North, what it meant and why there was a need for it. Jilly talked about equal rights for women. What caught Pat's attention was that she said the feminist movement was becoming too militant and that a lot of women were trying to be like men and losing their femininity when, in actual fact, they should be proud of it as it was part of their physical makeup. They should not have to apologise for it but they should try to make men realise that it is their brains and ability that should have them accepted as an equal partner – not the fact that they burned their bras and wore dungarees and hobnail boots.

She said that when she finished her degree she expected to get equal status with her male colleagues. She would get it, she said, because she'd worked hard for it and she would not have men look down their noses at her because they thought of her as being the little woman trying to play in a man's world. She said she didn't want to be in a man's world; she wanted to be in her own world with a decent job and a decent wage because she was entitled to it.

She told the meeting that it was about time that men looked past a woman's legs, bum and boobs and realised that they actually had brains and a lot to offer out there.

When she started to run down the militant feminist movement at the beginning she was booed and hissed, but within minutes she had the hall silent and listening to her every word and that included Pat. As he listened to her, he thought of his mother. How she ran the family with love and care and how she dealt with anything that went wrong in the home. She had taught herself carpentry from books and built numerous things around the house and did all the decorating. She didn't really need to do this but if it stopped Pat's father from worrying about extra expenses, then that's what his mother did.

He knew his mother came from a very privileged background and it wasn't as if she had been used to doing anything like this, but after his father qualified he wouldn't let her touch any of her money that had been left to her. He felt it was his job to provide for his family and that was the way it was.

Pat's father got a decent salary but it was by no means extravagant, so money had to be put by for the children's education from this. Mum could do whatever she liked with her money as long as it wasn't spent on providing day-to-day care for the family. She spent it on holidays every year and on special outfits for the kids at Christmas, birthdays and Easter, or special treats during the year.

Pat was thinking all this while Jilly talked and he knew she was right. His mother was a very intelligent woman and because she stayed at home to look after the family, it did not make her inferior. As a matter of fact, Pat sometimes thought his mother was more intelligent than his father, even though he was a qualified scientist. He seemed to be able to deal with only one thing but his mum seemed to be able to juggle dozens of things at the same time and they all seemed to work out right. These could range from the children's homework, to running to collect them from different classes, going to different meetings, paying bills and running the house.

He'd had many discussions with his mother on different issues and he was often surprised at her grasp and opinions on subjects he'd never even thought she had any interest in. If there was anything he wanted to discuss with her and she thought her knowledge was a bit sparse, she would read up on it and then decide what her own opinion was on the subject and they would debate it.

As far as Pat was concerned, his mother could go anywhere and hold her own in any company, whether socially or intellectually. As far as Jilly was concerned, she was getting no argument from Pat and he told her as much after the meeting.

In some ways he was very naive. He'd never really thought about women in the workplace and how they usually had to be twice as good as a man to be taken any way seriously. If a woman wanted to progress in a job and be promoted, she generally had to make a choice between either family or a career. In most cases at that time, the woman had to resign if she decided to get married and have children.

By the time he'd finished talking to Jilly that night, he'd learned a lot about women's rights that he'd never known or thought about.

What started off as a few words of congratulation from him to her ended up with them still talking over breakfast the next morning. Pat really admired Jilly's attitude to a lot of issues – he felt he could talk to her forever and also found himself laughing with her because she had a wicked sense of humour and wasn't afraid to laugh at herself or him. She also told him that he could sound very pompous when he was on his, as she called it, "soapbox".

He eventually had to tear himself away and attend to his own busy schedule. He left thinking that it had been an interesting interlude and nothing else. But as the days went by, he kept thinking of her and wondering what she was doing. Even then he never thought of getting in touch with her again. It wasn't until four weeks later when he was attending a dance to raise money for the civil rights movement that he met her again. He was talking to some people at the bar when he saw her. She was with some other people further along. He looked up, and straight into her eyes. He stopped talking and stood still for a few moments, and then walked off in mid-sentence towards her. She met him halfway.

He never even thought, he just said, "Would you like to leave?"

"I'll just get my coat," she answered.

They left the hotel and started to walk. It was a beautiful night. She slipped her hand into his and it felt so right to him.

They walked from the centre of Dublin out to Rathmines where Pat was living. Neither could remember what they talked about – it was nothing of real importance.

When they reached Pat's flat, they turned to each other and smiled. He opened the door and they walked in, and then both of them reached out to touch the other. To Pat it was such an intense moment when he looked at her. What he saw totally amazed him. She looked so beautiful.

He kissed her eyes slowly one by one, then her cheeks and neck. He wanted to feel and taste every piece of her. He slowly opened her blouse and kissed her shoulders and breasts. He wanted to ravish her there and then, but he didn't want to do it too quickly because he wanted to remember this moment forever.

The feeling that he had waited for this for a very long time was very clear to him. It was as though he was where he'd always wanted to be and with the one person who meant everything to him.

Pat had fallen in love and he knew it. They made love for hours. They couldn't stop touching each other. They would doze for a few minutes and then wake up and look at each other. Both were so surprised and so pleased to be where they were. They had finally met their soulmates. They didn't feel as though they needed to talk. Just to look into each other's eyes and touch each other seemed enough. Yet they wanted to say so much to each other. Pat held Jilly by the shoulder and looking into her eyes, he said, "I love you."

She replied, "I know, and I love you too."

They smiled and held each other tenderly.

As they lay together and watched the sunshine peep through the curtains, they felt as though this was the beginning of something wonderful. They didn't want to part. They talked on into the morning, deciding what they would do, and eventually decided that Jilly would move in with Pat. Once that was decided, both seemed to relax. It just seemed the right thing to do as neither wanted to be parted. Pat's flat was big enough for two, with a room they could turn into an office for their studying and committee work.

They got up, washed and dressed, and decided to go out for breakfast. Walking hand in hand along the street, they kept smiling and looking at each other, and stopping to kiss. Neither ate much.

They seemed to have so much to say to each other. The talk ranged from their families, to religion, Ireland and how much they loved it and back to each other.

Jilly was from Connemara and as she spoke, Pat could hear her affection for it. As she described her home and the area she came from, he could almost smell the sea, almost feel the mountain breeze and smell the heather. He had spent a few days in Achill when he was younger. His mother had insisted that they see and appreciate the beauty of their own country before they saw any other country.

He remembered a little village called Keel, where the sea washed up to the foot of the mountain and the sun was shining. There were fishing boats, narrow roads that ran along the shoreline and famine walls, and it felt as though you had stepped back about fifty years. He remembered the old men and women chatting to him being very helpful and good-humoured. It was one of those memories that he had stored very carefully in his memory and that he would take out and look at every once in a while. He had always intended to go back just to see if he had dreamed all of it or if it indeed was like he remembered. Many times over the past few summer holidays he had wanted to go, but he was afraid that if he did he would discover that it had only been a boy's illusion, a fantasy that could not be appreciated by the man.

He told Jilly this and she was really pleased. To her, Keel was a very special place. Her aunt lived there and she spent at least a fortnight there every year when she was a child, and still went two or three times a year. It was like being cut off from the rest of the world, where you could forget your troubles and just sleep, walk, swim and let the peace of the place wash over you and enjoy the helpfulness and the friendliness of the people.

Pat looked at Jilly and said, "What have you got to do today, can it be cancelled?"

"Now what are you up to?" she asked.

"Come on," he said, "humour me. Can it be cancelled?"

"Yes," she said.

"Do it, we're going to Keel. I want to be there with you. We'll pack an overnight bag and go. We'll come back tomorrow night but for now we are getting away from everyone and everything and we are just going to be together in the one spot we both loved. The sun is shining, we're in love and I feel crazy. Let's just go."

And he laughed out loud.

Jilly looked at him and laughed. "Yeah," she said, "let's do it," and she headed for the phone.

Pat really did feel as though he had gone crazy. He had about dozens of things to do but at this moment in time they didn't seem that important. The most important thing in his life at that moment was to spend time with Jilly.

Two minutes would cancel the lot, he thought. Everyone can be done without and the civil rights movement was not going to fall apart just because he didn't turn up for a few meetings for a day or two, or even a long weekend.

He was astounded at himself. He wasn't used to doing things on the spur of the moment. The last time he had probably done something as spontaneous as this would have been when he was still at school. Probably in short trousers! He didn't like to think it, but he was a very organised and controlled person.

When Jilly returned from making her phone calls, they went to her place to pick up some clothes and then to his to cancel all his commitments for the weekend, or as he said to "grab a few pairs of knickers" and then they closed the door and headed off for Achill.

They took Pat's car as it was in better condition than Jilly's old banger, and within a few hours they hit the island and were in Keel at the other side in no time. After booking in to a bed and breakfast, they headed off, walking around the headland for miles. It was beautiful. The sun was shining, the birds were singing and all was right with the world. They watched the wild sea crash in at the toes of the black mountain as the last rays of sun left the sky.

They called in on Jilly's aunt on the way back and Pat immediately took a great liking to her. She was uniquely dressed in clothes that had vestiges of other cultures to them. Embroidered jackets that raised memories of North Africa or maybe India, a skirt that could have come from Asia or maybe South America, scarves and shawls thrown over her shoulders reminiscent of Peru or Ecuador. She made silver jewellery, a lot of which dangled from her ears and wrists and even her hair. All around the cottage were pieces of pottery she had also made, with some wonderful paintings on it.

To Pat, she seemed really eccentric which was probably part of the fascination for him. She looked like an ageing hippie – all fringes, lace and jewellery. He thought she had a great face, with high cheekbones, a strong nose and skin almost without wrinkles. It was framed by a head of wavy grey hair.

After they had been chatting for a couple of hours, she looked at Pat and said, "I think I'm going to like you."

"Funnily enough," said Pat, "I think I'm going to like you too."

She mysteriously kept disappearing and not coming back for ages. Jilly said that she was probably feeding the chickens or taking the dog for a walk. She never said where she was going and didn't expect anyone else to feel that they had to explain themselves to her either. She was a truly free spirit.

That was why Jilly loved being with her. She was always allowed to do her own thing and no questions asked. There was another side to her that she loved – she was a great listener. You could talk to her for hours and just from the way she asked simple questions, you found that you had worked out problems that you couldn't see a solution to before, and she never judged.

Jo, as Jilly called her aunt, arrived back eventually with two bottles of homemade wine that she had made herself, which they opened when they got back to their guesthouse. They talked well into the night and were totally at peace.

The next two days passed as though in a dream. On the third evening, they called on Jo again to say goodbye and as they were leaving, she gave them another two bottles of her wine and said to Jilly at the door, "I like your friend; you two look after each other."

Pat smiled and bent and kissed Jo's cheek and she laughed and said, "I haven't been kissed by a young man in a long time!"

"Well, you should be kissed regularly by young and old men," laughed Pat.

"I like your thinking," laughed Jo in return.

During the journey home in the car, Jilly related her Aunt Jo's history.

She'd spent her life travelling and nursing, mostly in the Far East. She had trained in London although now she dabbled more in alternative medicine. A lot of her education in this field had come from women in isolated parts of the world, where they had to resort to natural remedies when supplies could not reach them because of bad weather, wars or rugged terrain.

She'd been in most of the African countries, in a kibbutz in Israel and various war-torn countries in Africa. She had once been married to a doctor and they had travelled the world together to many weird and wonderful places until eventually they had ended up in India, where he had died from a heart attack.

She'd carried on for a few years working in foreign countries but it wasn't the same, so one day she suddenly decided she was going home. She bought the little cottage in Keel and continued to do a little bit of holistic healing and dabble in alternative medicine if someone came to her.

Jilly said that her attitude was, "You had to do what you could for the people because that was what God put you here for, to help your fellow human being. If you didn't then you weren't much of a human being yourself!"

"Although her idea of God or the Goddess would not be exactly what others might agree with," laughed Jilly.

Jo now very seldom left Achill except about once a year when she felt she should "go and see a bit of the rest of the country", so she headed off with her rucksack on her back in the battered minibus she owned. A few weeks later, "newsy" cards would start arriving from all over the country. She always seemed to end up either at a music session which lasted for days – where she was surely giving her rather large repertoire of indigenous songs or expressing stories from all over the world – or at a village where some real quaint characters lived that she had to visit, or maybe a commune of New Age Travellers.

You could never tell where she would find herself. She once ended up in a convent with nuns, doing a retreat even though she had very little time for organised religion. She claimed she had cut out the middle men and gone straight to the Goddess herself. When asked about the retreat, she said it was so peaceful there she decided to stay for a few days, and the food wasn't bad either.

She always landed home with two or maybe three people in tow who stayed until they found their peace and often came back to visit.

Jilly told Pat he would be amazed at the people who came to visit Jo from all over the world. They ranged in colour from black, red, yellow to white. Ministers of state from countries very few had ever heard of. There were men and women with full national costumes and clergy of many religions.

Jilly said that in any given week Jo would receive and write at least twenty letters. Even though she didn't have a radio, she knew most of what was going on in the world. She got it first hand from those who were involved in whatever was happening throughout the world.

As Pat looked at Jilly, he thought that now he knew where she got her confidence and character from. She was her own woman and he thought that her Aunt Jo's influence had a lot to do with it.

Listening to Jilly talk, Pat realised that she didn't really need him in her life to make it complete. She was a very sound, well-rounded person on her own, but she wanted him in her life and that really pleased him.

The few days they spent in Achill were the happiest he could ever remember spending with anyone.

When they arrived back in Dublin, they collected some books and clothes from her apartment and she moved into Pat's flat. Now that they had made the decision to be together permanently they had to settle down, get back to normal and go to college. Both were determined to qualify, go to their respective meetings and just get on with life in general.

Neither expected or wanted the other to give up anything they were involved in but both cut back a little so they could spend more of their spare time together. They also decided that when either had a night off and the other had to go out to a meeting or protest, then they would accompany the other. He helped her organise meetings and paint placards for her feminist movement activities. She became involved in the civil rights movement with him.

Jilly went to Belfast with Pat to meet his family, who all grew to love her. They fully approved of Pat's choice of partner and were always teasing them about tying the knot.

"You're only looking for a big day out," Pat would tell them.

Jilly used to laugh and say, "Don't worry, I'll make him marry me and give you all a great day out!"

Pat visited Connemara and met Jilly's family. The story was identical there, and the teasing the same.

They met Chris and his numerous girlfriends and often went out with him. He would travel to and from meetings with them or would often invite himself around for dinner, especially if he knew Jilly was cooking. The three of them got on very well. They kept trying to pair him off with different women but they never lasted.

One Friday evening, Chris was heading home to Donegal and told Pat that he wouldn't be coming back to Dublin until Tuesday afternoon. Jilly and Pat were going to Belfast for the weekend and were then going to Derry on Sunday for a march. All three decided to meet up beforehand. All were getting worried about the way things had been going at the marches lately. There had been a lot of aggression from the RUC and the British soldiers.

None of them felt any fear about going to the march that Sunday – after all, it was a civil rights march and they had every right to march. Nobody but nobody believed that things would get as bad as they did, or that the day would go down in history as one of the greatest abuses of human and civil rights.

They met Chris just outside of Derry and were late arriving at the starting point, and there were a few hundred there already. Finding themselves at the back of the crowd, some of the other people pushed their way up towards the middle but Pat, Jilly and Chris stayed where they were as there was more room. As the march got on the move, they walked along with the crowd chatting about their week and what they had planned for the following one. Just everyday chit-chat.

Nothing gave them any indication of the mayhem that would erupt very soon. People alongside them were walking on naturally and they just meandered along, wondering where they would go for something to eat, when they heard the bangs.

Chris and Pat looked at each other in shock and confusion, and then pandemonium broke out. People were screaming and running all over the place.

Pat grabbed Jilly and ran with her, away from the crowd. She kept shouting, "What's happening, what's happening?"

"They're shooting at us, run like hell!" said Pat. "Jesus Christ! They're shooting at us. Oh God, Jilly! They're shooting into the crowd!"

"They wouldn't," said Jilly. "They couldn't do something like that!"

"They have, I'm telling you, they have!" roared Pat.

They ran on. Pat just wanted to get her away, to make sure she was safe. He was terrified that something would happen to her. He was also worried because they had lost Chris in the crowd.

They found themselves running along a street when a woman came to the door of a house and called them in. They ran in and realised there were a lot of other people there already.

"God! What has happened; did they really shoot into the crowd?" asked Pat.

One old man, who was handing around tea, looked at him and said, "God bless you son, weren't you expecting it? They don't like it when we stand up to them and step out of our ghettos."

Pat looked at him, shocked.

"Ach son!" said the old man. "They've been doing it all over the years. You didn't expect them to stop just because smart young fellows like you joined the protesters?"

"But that's murder!" exclaimed Pat.

"Not to them, it's not. They just think of it as controlling and culling the vermin. We're not intelligent human beings to them – we're just lowlife. Haven't you read your Irish history, son?" said the old man.

"But this is 1972," said Pat.

"Arrah son! It doesn't matter. The British authorities will only stop when we prove to them that they cannot treat us like that anymore."

"And how are we going to do that?" asked Pat.

"I'm afraid we're just going to have to treat like with like and take to the gun ourselves again," said the old man.

"But isn't there any other way?" cried Pat, for he couldn't visualise himself using a gun against anyone.

"No son, I don't think there is," sighed the old man.

The radio was on and they were all waiting to hear what had actually happened. When the newsflash came on, they heard that the British soldiers had opened fire into the crowd and some people had been shot dead. They didn't know how many yet.

Pat and Jilly were in shock. They couldn't believe it.

"Oh Christ!" shouted Pat. "Chris! Where's Chris?"

"Oh my God!" said Jilly. "We forgot about him."

"When did you last see him?" asked the old man.

"When everyone started to run," said Pat, "we got separated."

"Where were you supposed to meet up?" he asked Pat.

"If we got separated, we were to meet back at the cars when the march was over."

"Right! Where's the car? I'll send one of the boys to the car to see if he's there and get him back here."

Pat agreed, as he didn't know where to start looking for him and was still too shocked to want to drive. All he kept thinking was that if they had been earlier arriving at the march, Jilly could have been one of those lying dead now. He couldn't bear the thought.

Eventually Chris arrived and he was delighted to see that Pat and Jilly were safe.

He asked to use the phone to ring Colly and their relatives to let them know that they were safe and to check to see if all those he knew who were attending the march had checked in.

After he spoke to her, Colly said she would ring around and check with everyone.

When this was done, they decided that they should head home. They got into their cars and all headed back to Dublin, totally shocked. They could not wait to get out of Derry that day.

Pat and Jilly were very quiet on their way home. They seemed to be still in shock or lost deep in their own thoughts. Pat and Jilly held hands for most of the journey. Every now and then she would lift his hand and kiss it as though to say, "Thank God you're alive."

They arrived home, exhausted by the whole trauma.

Even back at the flat, there didn't seem to be much to say. They hugged each other a lot and went to bed and held each other.

During the night, Pat heard Jilly cry out. He turned to her and held her and said, "It's just a bad dream, darling! Go back to sleep."

He was very angry that she had been put through such a horrifying experience and couldn't get out of his head the thought of all those who had lost their lives there on the streets of Derry. At some time during the night, after tossing and turning for hours, Pat fell asleep.

But the horror for Pat was only starting. When he awoke in the morning and tried to wake Jilly, there was no response. She was never going to wake again in this life and was lying cold and dead beside him.

He shook her and shouted her name but he got no response. He lifted her body and begged her to answer him but she would never speak again. He ran to the phone to ring the ambulance. He couldn't stand up; his legs had given up under him. He knew she was dead but his mind could not accept it.

He rang Chris frantically, who raced over but it was too late. Both men were stunned when the ambulance arrived. They watched her body being removed from the flat on a stretcher and still they couldn't believe it. Where had the bundle of energy, intelligence, wit and love gone?

Pat said he had to ring Jilly's family and tell them what had happened. He also had to ring his own family. How was he going to tell any of them? Chris took over and decided he would have to do this as Pat didn't seem able to string two words together without breaking down.

Gradually the parents arrived in Dublin, both Jilly's and Pat's, and took over the arrangements for the funeral. No one could take it in. It seemed so surreal; how could this happen? She was a healthy young woman!

Much later, an autopsy revealed it was a massive heart attack. The doctor told Pat that there must have been a problem with her heart already that hadn't been detected, but Pat never believed that. All he knew was that the British soldiers in Derry had killed his only love.

He went through the next week in a trance; everyone did what they could for him but no one seemed to be able to get through to him. This was the most devastating thing that had ever happened to Pat. To him it was so traumatic that he just couldn't get his head around it. One minute he had everything to live for, and now, absolutely nothing. What went before or would come after didn't matter, anything that was good and worth living for was gone.

The funeral took place in Jilly's hometown, and Pat and Chris travelled from Dublin with the coffin. Pat found it impossible to believe she was gone.

In his head he could still hear her voice and he would remember all the things they had planned for the future. Then he would remember that they had no future together, and that was the worst part of it. Everything that was to come was to be with him and Jilly together, and now all that stretched ahead of him was a vast emptiness and no Jilly. It was like his brain was screaming and all he wanted to do was to find a switch to turn it off. He kept remembering her vitality, her laughter, her teasing, their walks together, their lovemaking, and he couldn't equate this with the person in the coffin or believe that all this was gone. How could something so vital and alive be gone, dead, never to speak to him again?

Pat watched as they buried her body and then he cried tears like a baby. As they started, he turned and stumbled away from the grave. He staggered through the graveyard sobbing, eventually finding himself sitting at the side of the church on a large tombstone. He was shattered and all he wanted to do was to stop thinking.

"Dear God! Just give me something to stop me thinking," he cried. "Oh God! How am I going to go on? I can't deal with this."

Chris found him sitting there and was very shocked at the state he was in. He could never have conceived the Pat he knew falling apart like this. He didn't know what to do.

Let him cry, he thought. *He needs to get it out of his system.*

He stayed where he was for a few minutes and just kept an eye on him. His heart ached for his friend but he felt totally useless.

A little while later, he went to him and sat beside him, put his arm around him and held him.

"What am I going to do without her, Chris?" asked Pat.

They sat there for quite a while until Aunt Jo found them.

She took Pat's arm, pulled him up off the gravestone and told him, "You're coming with me."

She then turned to Chris and told him to tell everyone that she and Pat would not be going to the funeral dinner, they were going to Keel.

"I think you're right, he's not up to dealing with people right now," said Chris.

Pat walked along like a zombie to the car with Jo and got in. He just didn't seem capable of making any decisions and seemed glad that they were being made for him. They drove to Achill in almost total silence. He didn't notice the journey; nothing seemed to be getting through to him. Jo spoke to him a few times but he did not seem to hear her. It did not matter where he went now that there was nothing of importance left in his life.

They parked at Jo's little cottage and went in. She boiled the kettle and filled a hot water bottle and brought him up to bed. When she had settled him in, she brought him a drink of some concoction she had made for shock, which she said would make him sleep. Pat drank it because all he wanted to do was to stop thinking, and sleep would help him to do that. He slept on and off for three days, with Jo bringing him something to eat and drink.

He stayed with her for the next three weeks. She got in touch with the college and explained the situation, and he got compassionate leave until he was ready to return. He did nothing much every day, except walk the island and talk to her about anything but Jilly. She tried broaching the subject a few times but he either walked away or changed the subject.

When he was there about ten days, she woke up one night and heard him crying in his room. This had happened a few times and she had let him cry. She hadn't wanted to intrude. This night she decided to go to him. He was sitting at his window just looking out, with the tears streaming down his face. She pulled up a chair beside him and held his hand.

"Let her go, Pat," she said. "Let her rest."

"She shouldn't be dead, Jo," he said, "and she wouldn't be if she hadn't been at that march with me."

"Pat! You don't know that, it could have happened anyway. She had a faulty heart."

"No!" he shouted. "It was those bastards shooting innocent protesters that killed her."

"What happened that Sunday was dreadful and there is no excusing it, but Jilly's heart had a defect and that's what killed her," she pleaded.

"But don't you see if it hadn't been for the shooting we might have found out about the defect and got something done about it in the future, and she could have lived a long life. It was the shock, and her realising that the British thought they could mow down the Irish people and get away with it that killed her."

"Pat, you are very angry and that is natural, and you are looking for someone to blame but you've got to believe that some things are meant to be."

"Yes!" said Pat. "I believe that Jilly died so that my eyes would be opened to what was happening in my own country and for me to do something about it. Now that is what I'm going to dedicate my life to. Making Ireland a free country, free of English oppression, free from brutes who think they can open fire on a street and murder innocent Irish people and who think they can do what they want in my country. I'm going to show them they can't."

"Maybe you're right, your work for the civil rights movement is very important, and positive thought will carry you through this. When you qualify you will be able to do a lot more but a positive attitude is what you need now," she replied.

But Pat was not thinking of the civil rights movement, he was thinking of the old man's words, "We have to treat like with like."

He now believed that the old man was right. The more he thought about it, the more he realised that people who thought that they could shoot into a march of ordinary people and get away with it had a lot to learn, and there was only one way to teach them – by playing them at their own game.

Up until now he never believed that the situation merited guns. He knew that Chris believed that was the way it was going to end up and that he was, at this moment, involved in moving guns around the country. But not until that minute did he believe that it was the only solution.

It was against his nature to even contemplate lifting a gun to kill another person. To him they had seemed like macho games that some men felt obliged to play. Now he could see no other way.

Chris had told him that protesting on its own would not stop the British. He said it would take a lot more and that what was needed was an efficient army of men and women who would do what it took to rid the country of the injustices meted out by the British to the Irish people.

Now here was one more recruit. One that would have never been recruited was it not for the brutality of the British Army. As far as he was concerned, now he was going to remove every Brit and every one of their sympathisers from Ireland. He was going to get himself trained and he was going to be the most effective soldier that the IRA ever had. The rest of his life was going to be spent avenging Jilly's death.

He didn't tell this to Jo. He looked at her, smiled and said, "Yes! That's what I need, a positive attitude."

When she looked at him, she felt a shiver run down her spine. It wasn't peaceful acceptance she saw on his face but revenge and hatred. She squeezed his hand and said she would make tea. She was very worried.

What have they done to him, she thought.

Pat left Keel a few days later and headed to Belfast. He didn't want to see Chris or any of his old friends. He had a job to do and he wanted no distractions or anyone to tell him he was wrong. He felt in his heart he was right. Not only that, but now he had a purpose back in his life which was something Jilly's death had taken from him.

He knew a few good men involved in the IRA in Belfast and he was going to see them. He would talk to them and see what he could do. He was sure that they would be glad of another recruit.

Surprisingly for him, he did not get the reception that he expected.

He was really shocked at first by what he was told when he met the men. They listened to him and discussed his work up until then with him, and they then told him to go back to Dublin and finish his degree and sit quiet for a while.

This was not what he wanted to do; he couldn't have cared less about his Law studies. All he wanted was to get a gun and blow every British soldier out of Northern Ireland. They told him that he was no good to them with that attitude. They did not want a hothead on their hands, but if he went back to Dublin and did what he was told and waited until things died down a bit, they would send for him, and by then he would be more useful to them.

They explained to him that if he did this and kept out of politics, stopped his civil rights involvement and lowered his profile, then there would be no attention paid to him by the British Army and afterwards he could do what he wanted without drawing attention to himself.

He thought about all they had said to him for a few days while he visited his family and finally could see the sense it made. He eventually decided to go back to Dublin and back to university.

Initially he felt frustrated but gradually began to realise that this was the best plan not only for the IRA, but also for him. He would keep a low profile and he would not only pass his exams but he would be trained in the use of guns and guerrilla warfare by the time he would pass. He would also know a lot more about what it would take to remove the British from Ireland.

He had a lot of learning ahead of him and he looked forward to it. He was obsessed with his plan and how he would carry it out. He had to make himself into someone who was beyond reproach, and a good student was the beginning. The rest would follow.

He stopped attending meetings and started to study very seriously everything he wanted or felt he needed to learn. His university studies came first, and after that it was anything he could get his hands on about warfare from all over the world. Gradually his pain at losing Jilly eased, but never went away. He now felt that he had something positive to work towards, a real purpose in life.

At first his thinking was fanatical but as the pain eased, so did the craziness. He began to think more clearly and intelligently. He knew that if the plan was to work, it had to be planned out carefully and methodically. No stupid heroics. Each operation had to be planned to the last detail.

They were up against a trained army and intelligence way beyond what the IRA had, so they had to use what they had to the best of their ability. He needed training and discipline and he was going to find out where he could get it.

At first, he didn't tell Chris what he was up to. He wanted to get it all sorted out in his head first and there was also the fact that he knew that he wouldn't approve. He knew that he would tell him that he was doing it for the wrong reasons. He also knew that he had been worrying about him – not because he thought he was falling apart, but because he wasn't and because he was so controlled.

After he'd come back to Dublin, Chris had kept calling him to see if he was alright. After Pat had given up all his connections to the civil rights movement, Chris began to really worry. Each time he'd called to the flat, he'd found him studying or going to classes and apparently getting on with his life as though everything was alright with the world and nothing had happened. He didn't know what to think.

He couldn't equate this with the Pat he had last seen falling apart in the churchyard. He had known him most of his life and he just knew that there had to be some explanation for his behaviour and the total lack of emotion.

After a while, Pat began to open up to Chris and gradually told him what he was doing. By this time, he had his mind made up about how he felt and what he planned to do. He was now sure he was doing the right thing.

They would talk into the night about the situation in Ireland and what could be done. Initially, Chris wanted nothing to do with the plan, but gradually he began to realise that Pat wasn't going at it like a lunatic but was methodically planning a strategy which might work.

Over the next few years, it came to the level that it now was no longer a theoretical plan but very much a reality. Each of them, in their own way, had come to the conclusion that there was no alternative but all-out war and they felt no guilt about it. All they saw were the injustices that had been meted out to the Irish people down through the ages, and the only solution was now being worked out very carefully. The IRA were possibly getting the best recruits they had ever had.

After a while, Pat started to talk about Jilly. He told Chris that at first, all he could think of was revenge for her death. Gradually, he explained, his thinking became more calculated and it eventually came to him that what he was thinking of was stupid and would not help himself, Jilly or the Irish people.

As his thinking changed, so too did his reasoning, and eventually he knew that he wanted to become involved because it was the right thing to do. He felt that his country needed people like him who were proud of what they were and where they came from and were not ashamed to say so. Neither was he ashamed to fight for what he thought of as the very basic rights of the Irish people. A decent education, a proper job, a decent place to live and that if he chose to live in East or West Belfast, then that was where he had the right to choose to live. He should not have to worry about intimidation or being run out of it or being murdered because some Protestant paramilitary gang did not like it.

"In fact," Pat said, "I believe that Jilly died to show me what I should do. To me, her death has now served a purpose and this is it, this is why she died. I have finished my education as I planned, and now I'm qualified with a good job. Nobody knows what I get up to in my spare time. It's ideal. I am going to fight the English in whatever way I can."

Chris once turned to Pat and very thoughtfully and quietly said, "I don't know what to think about what you are doing. I have thought how you now think all my life, and in a way I have always known that the situation would come to this point for me one day. I knew that if things got bad, I would want to be involved. But I'm so used to you being a pacifist and taking the softly-softly approach to everything that now I'm a bit worried. A turned pacifist can be a very dangerous person. Like a loose cannon."

Pat laughed and said, "My way of thinking now is not fanatical or out of control, it is calculated and thorough, and what's more important, I know I'm right. I believe those men in Belfast were right to make me go back and finish my education and cool down. My thinking was all out of control then and I needed the time to get used to the pain. Now I'm ready although I have probably been better educated in a lot more subjects than they had foreseen, but I will be of more use to them now in more ways than one."

Pat had come out top of his class. But he also travelled all over the world to different places he had heard Jo speak about and where she had lived while a war was going on, and he talked to different bands of rebels about their strategies. A lot were just hill or jungle fighters but he learned different strategies from a lot of them.

He had hardened up and was physically very fit, but mentally he had changed. If he wasn't exactly obsessed with his plans he became very determined about them.

Finishing university, he accepted a position with a firm of solicitors near the Border. Even this was calculated. He wanted a firm that was as near to the Border as possible, who dealt with those affected by the Troubles and had a leaning towards Republicanism although not outright rebels. He couldn't be seen to associate with blatant IRA sympathisers. He needed to protect his cover.

He travelled to Belfast every weekend to go home, but often staying only for a couple of hours before going on to his secret paramilitary activities. He had returned many times over the years to see the Belfast men he had originally spoken to after Jilly's death. Through them, he made many useful contacts, all the time keeping a low profile and not telling anyone too much.

Many nights were spent in the little houses on the Falls Road in the small sculleries around a warm range or a kitchen table. Many cups of tea and bottles of Guinness were drunk with young and old men standing or sitting around, discussing what could be done. Through this interaction, Pat got to know what was happening in the North and the thinking of the people. He also got to know who to trust and who had a loose mouth.

After some time, he eventually took his courage in his hands and decided to put his trust in one man whom he knew and who had a solid, trustworthy reputation. Liam O'Malley had been involved in the civil rights movement from the beginning, and similar to Chris, he had decided to support the IRA. He had been actively involved with them for a few years. Pat told him what he was planning and Liam was surprised at his dedication and knowledge, and agreed to help him. When he heard what Pat had been doing over the previous few years, he told him that his service would be greatly appreciated.

Through him, Pat joined the IRA, training recruits. One or two of the top men got to know him over the years and were impressed with his abilities. He worked hard with a committed attitude and a vision of what he wanted to achieve, and he moved quickly up the ranks. He was an excellent leader and marksman.

At one point he became a sniper. This lone situation suited Pat. He would take off on his own, pick a strategic position and target an army patrol, and expel two or three shots at them and disappear. This was a sure-fire way to create panic in the British camp. The security forces could deal with a bomb or even volleys of shots from a group, but a lone gunman was harder to track, especially when he would only let off two or three shots, most very accurately, and then disappear. He rode a motorbike and was gone before they realised what had happened, and he could have left two or three soldiers dead in the meantime.

He never thought twice about the rights or the wrongs of it. He was a soldier and this was war. As far as he was concerned, every time he shot a soldier he was shooting one of Jilly's murderers and the murderers of all those other innocent people who lay on the streets of Derry.

For the next few years, he lived this double life. He would go on holiday to the continent and end up in Libya or Syria in training camps, or arranging for the shipment of arms. He became an expert on places and people, where he could get false passports and papers done and find people who he could get to act as couriers. He also became an expert on disguises.

Pat was commander of a few units in Northern Ireland. He both trained and commanded them. There were a few good and dedicated men running the IRA at this time, men with ideals and principles, and they had their finger on the pulse of everything that was happening. But over the next couple of years, a lot of them were shot or grew too old for active involvement and retired. Gradually, as these men disappeared, the same security wasn't in place and it became apparent to Pat that a lot of information was getting out, and a lot of the double agents or traitors were impossible to find.

Men's lives were being put at risk and there didn't seem to be any way to stop it. The IRA had tried to stop information getting out and had watched various people they suspected of leaking it, but most of these were cleared. Some guys that were suspected of passing on information had been executed, but afterwards it was apparent they had executed the wrong men.

Now it seemed that every avenue they went down, they drew a blank. It was getting too dangerous. Pat started looking around for another way to run the war against the British. Another way for him, that is.

Up until then, he had been very careful at concealing his identity. The dark glasses, collar up, scarf around the neck and beret did a good job. Very few people knew very much about him. He was just known as the commander and any questions about him were discouraged. Since he had joined, he only ever had close contact with a few of the top men.

It was well known that there was this top marksman and commander in their midst, but his exact identity remained a mystery to most and it was guarded from the top down. The units he trained accepted him. These included some of the top operators who then went on to train others under them. This man with a beret, dark glasses and combat gear was someone they were proud to have trained under, and the mystery of his identity just added to his legend. They accepted what he was; he did not welcome close scrutiny or intimacy of any sort, so no one tried. He was the true professional, there to put the troops through their paces and get out again. Those who tried to question him all learned very quickly to back off. Pat knew that the success of his work depended on his identity being kept secret.

At around this time, he and Chris got together and discussed the leakage of information and wondered what they would do about it. Many nights were taken up with discussions on different strategies, but nothing seemed foolproof. It was around this time that Chris talked to him about Colly and her plan for a secret unit.

"Colly has been saying the same thing for months and has been trying to work out a way to stop the security forces getting their hands on information. I think she has come up with a plan that may work," said Chris.

At first, Pat laughed at this. He wasn't a chauvinist, but he couldn't exactly imagine a wee woman in Donegal being an expert on guerrilla warfare. Nevertheless, he was very curious and he knew Chris definitely believed in this woman, and he was no fool.

The more they talked about her, the more he wanted to meet her. Who was she? What was her background? What did she do for a living? What was her interest in the struggle in Northern Ireland? What made her tick? Chris told him all he knew about her which was practically her life story, and as he had been in almost constant attendance for most of it, he knew it well.

Pat was very sceptical when he heard of her background. She sounded much too soft for a good operator. Business and IT specialist? He didn't think so! He pictured long manicured nails and designer suits.

Not exactly how he imagined a rebel operative!

"Stories from Granny's knee do not make a good fighter. She's living in a dream world. She couldn't survive in the world we are talking about," he told Chris.

Chris argued with Pat saying, "You don't know this woman! She's as tough as any man I know and a lot stronger mentally. She may look like a doll, but this doll is made of steel."

He told him of the ideas that she had and how she wanted to be involved. He explained how Colly saw her role as the sweet young woman on a deadly mission, above suspicion. Who would think she could be a bomber?

After a while and a lot of arguing, Pat gave in and agreed to meet Colly, but being cautious he wanted more time to think about it. He knew that if he went with her ideas, he would have to be able to trust her with his life and he would be responsible for sending all of them into very dangerous situations.

After a couple of weeks, he finally decided it was worth taking the chance. It was a good idea and he couldn't come up with anything better himself, and he was getting frustrated. He had to be able to control what was happening and this was one way of doing it.

They could create their own unit in Donegal with himself as the only contact with the other higher command units. No one outside the group would know who was involved and Pat would only report to one man.

When he decided that he had better meet Colly if the plan was to be realised, he knew he had better get a move on. Coincidentally, it was around this time that he attended a meeting in Belfast, where he recognised her name. He asked around to check if it was her, as there weren't many with a name like hers, and he arranged to bump into her after the meeting.

As he watched her sit at the meeting, he could see how cautious she was. He had known what she had been through up until then from Chris, but even though Chris had tried to explain what she was like, he still expected something different. He wasn't quite sure what – possibly someone less vibrant looking. To Pat, she looked very glamorous, with her cascading fall of auburn hair, her white shirt, jeans and blazer. She certainly didn't look like someone whose ambition in life was to blow every British soldier who ever set foot in Ireland to kingdom come.

After the short few words he had with her following the meeting, he concocted a plan to see what she was really made of and got Chris to get her to attend the training session in the Leitrim Mountains. The rest, as they say, is history.

Chapter Eight

Christopher Cassidy was born in London, to Irish parents. When he was younger this always annoyed him, especially when Colly used to call him an English brat, jokingly.

His father worked in a travel agency and his mother worked as a secretary. She was originally from Donegal and his father from Belfast. Both had very strong Republican connections. Both sets of grandfathers had been involved in the Old IRA. In a way, it was a bit like Colly's background, with none of their parents seeing a role for themselves in the struggle for independence today. It was as if they thought the last generation had tried and failed, so what was the point of them trying.

When Chris was two years old, his father decided to come back to Belfast and open his own travel agency. There were four children in Chris's family. He was the second youngest. He had a younger sister born after they returned to Belfast and two older brothers.

When the agency opened, his mother worked in it part-time with his father. Gradually, the business started to prosper. More and more Irish people were starting to take holidays abroad and there were very few travel agencies to cater for the demand at the time. As the business improved, unfortunately the marriage began to deteriorate. As Chris's mother said, "Sometimes when making money becomes your main priority, what your first priority should be, like relationships, gets forgotten about."

Gradually, their arguments got so bad they decided to separate. It was done in the old Irish way of a lot of broken marriages. They bought a house in Donegal for Chris's mother and she came back to live in Ballyshannon. His father moved in over the shop and their house in Belfast was sold. To all intents and purposes, they were still married but just lived in different places.

The boys stayed with their father during the week and went to school in Belfast. They would travel to Donegal to be with their mother at weekends and during holidays.

They came to live on the same road as Colly's grandmother and that is how they all became friends. Her Nan's house became like a second home to Chris, who would call in and chat to her even when Colly wasn't there. His memories as a child were something similar to Colly's. He remembered sitting on Nan's step and eating homemade bread and jam, and helping her tidy the garden and burning rubbish. He always remembered her talking to him and asking about his day at school and who his friends were now. She didn't talk to him like other adults did, as though he was stupid. It was as though she really wanted to know if he was doing alright, and that what he said was really important. Chris always claimed that her Nan respecting him and his opinions from when he was very young was the reason he grew into the confident man he was.

As far as he and Colly were concerned, they were practically inseparable. If Chris had a choice, he would have stayed in Donegal permanently. His mother felt that he needed a father's hand in his rearing. He often asked Nan to talk to his mum about it, but she always said he had to speak to his mother, and that it was up to his mother and father how they wanted him reared. She could not interfere. They fell out for a while over this but he didn't stay away for long. Within a couple of days he was back on the front doorstep with his bread and jam and all his questions, and was wandering through the garden raking up leaves here and deadheading flowers there as he chatted to Nan and Colly.

Even though they were separated, his parents eventually became very good friends. His mother would return to stay in Belfast with his father during the year if she wanted to do some shopping, or if there was somewhere the children needed to go, she would be there to bring them. His father came to Donegal three or four times a year and always at Christmas. If Chris's father was short of help in the shop, Chris's mother would spend a few days with him until he sorted the problem out.

They never got divorced – it never was an option and neither seemed to want to. They got on a lot better living apart than they did living together. They often went out socially, both in Belfast and Donegal, and were accepted as a normal couple. If there were any family celebrations, they attended together. As a matter of fact, they probably had more respect for each other than most married couples who lived together.

Chris used to ask his parents why they didn't live together when they seemed to get on so well and really seemed to care for each other. His father told him that some people could not take the pressure of living together and all the responsibilities this entailed, and that although he loved his mother and she loved him, they were better off not living too close to each other. As it was, there were less rows and the family were all happier. But nothing is perfect, and when Chris would be older, he could decide for himself where he wanted to live, but until then Chris's father and mother would make the decisions.

Later, as Chris got older, his father told him that when he and Chris's mother first split up, he decided that was the end of his marriage and that he was going to get on with life. In the first few years, he had what he called a few "skirmishes" with other women, and they had all fallen short of what he'd had with Chris's mother. After a while, when the anger and bad feelings between them had died down and they began talking to each other, he realised that he really loved her. He also realised that if living apart and only seeing each other now and again was the only way to make their marriage work, then that was what he would do. He also said that they now had a more trusting relationship than other marriages he knew.

His mother's thinking was that they were there for each other when they were needed and that they didn't have to live in each other's pockets to do this. It took them about two years after they split to get to this point of the relationship.

Their obvious problem was that they were two very strong and independent personalities. Neither would back down and both were very fond of expressing their opinions. Once they realised this and that they had to work together to rear their four children, the fighting stopped. Being sane and intelligent people, they stood back, looked at the situation and decided to do the best they could.

Chris was proud of his parents. He never heard either his mother or his father saying a wrong word about the other and he was never afraid to speak to one about the other. He was taught by them to respect people even if you did not agree with them. The only thing that Chris had ever thought might have been slightly wrong in his home life was that he was expected to be independent too soon. He was taught to look after himself at an early age and was then expected to get on with it.

Somewhere along the line, he began to tell his parents less and less about what was happening in his life or what he thought. He instinctively knew they would not approve of the opinions he was developing. There were some things that he wanted to keep to himself and work out for himself. Things he didn't want to be dissected in minute detail.

At the beginning, when he went to Nan's house, he would tell his mum all he had seen and heard there. He would tell her the stories that Nan had told him and she would listen, but would then argue different aspects of them. This somehow ruined the stories for Chris. His fantasy that he had woven around them was shattered and ruined.

When he listened to the stories Nan told, he, like Colly, was out there with the freedom fighters in his imagination. He and Colly were at the head of this great imaginary army running through the bogs and fields of Ireland, helping to free their great land. They were wandering the country lanes looking for assistance from trusted rural people who put them up in hay lofts, or they were ambushing British soldiers. When they were younger, they would re-enact these scenes in Nan's garden or go out through the local countryside with pieces of wood for rifles.

As a child, Chris read of Fionn mac Cumhaill, Cú Chulainn and the De Danann. Later, it was the heroes of the Easter Rising. He and Colly would buy books, exchange them with each other and then discuss them with Nan.

In their teens, they would go off hiking into the country and talk about the people who walked the same land that they were walking, hundreds of years before. They would talk about the famine and the people who were so hungry they had to eat grass, how they were starved and persecuted by the British and how they had to work so hard to survive on their little farms and give most of their products to the landlord. They spoke of how the Old IRA had to go on the run from area to area and house to house like Colly's grandfather, and how they were hounded by the English and a lot of them shot.

Although Chris knew that both of his grandparents had Republican involvements and that he could probably have been able to tell his parents these stories, this was not something that he felt he could share with his parents so he learned to keep it to himself.

As he grew older, the dream grew with him, but when he reached his teens while he was around Belfast, that dream began to seem very real to him. He had spent a lot of time on the Falls Road and in Ardoyne growing up with his school pals, and had heard all the stories of abuse and segregation. Unlike Chris, Pat had not realised until much later in life exactly how bad things were for people in Northern Ireland.

Chris had seen and listened to stories of the deprivation and oppression in the houses in the Catholic areas long before the civil rights marches, and had always thought that there must be something more that could be done to give the Catholics a better quality of life.

Earlier than 1968 or 1969, at the civil rights marches he listened to different people talk about the situation, and this had a great influence on Chris's thinking. After some of these discussions, his anger would rise because he felt no one was doing anything and that everyone should be out there, fighting for their rights.

"We are lying down and being walked on by the Loyalists in the North," he would shout to anyone who would listen.

"What do you want us to do, son?" they would say. "The British have a big army; we have about twenty guns in the whole of Northern Ireland."

"Why the hell don't they get up and protest? And if that doesn't work, then we should all take to the streets and fight for the justice we know is our right."

If he had his way, every man, woman and child would be out there protesting against every injustice that was ever perpetrated by the Loyalist community on the Catholics. When the civil rights marches started in Northern Ireland, it was a huge relief to Chris.

At last, he thought, *the people are getting their strength and are standing up and being counted.*

But in his heart he knew that civil protests were not going to be enough. He knew the history of the English towards the Irish. He knew they had complete contempt for the Irish fight for equality and justice.

"It isn't going to be enough to tell them that they can't stay in Ireland and treat the Irish with the contempt that they do. They have to be shown that they can't do it," he said to anyone who would listen. He was often laughed about as the "wee Republican hothead".

He talked to Pat about the way he felt and they often argued into the night about different actions and strategies that could be used. At that time, Pat thought that Chris was too fanatical or just a dreamer who wanted everything to be wonderful.

"Life is not like that," he would tell him.

He thought that Chris envisaged himself as a fictional action hero who would sort out the Irish problems in one clean swoop. He would often laugh at his plans and tell him to be realistic. There had to be other ways of dealing with these problems rather than taking to the gun. It seemed too extreme to him. You could not just shoot another person to get what you wanted.

When the marches started, Chris and Pat went together because this was something they believed was the thing to do – to get the people on the streets.

"People power would get the British out of Ireland once and for all!" Pat would say. Chris doubted it.

Pat was glad to support the movement and saw this as a way to look after Chris. He thought he was a bit too hot-headed and would get himself in trouble if there wasn't someone there to curb his enthusiasm. It was also a way to spend time with him as a friend.

As the months went by and they became more involved in the civil action, they would discuss all the things that Pat was finding out about the Catholic situation in the North. Chris would look at Pat and say, "I tried to tell you but you wouldn't listen. Your eyes and ears were totally shut. You only saw what you wanted to see."

Even though they were good friends, they knew that they couldn't expect the other to believe in every issue as deeply as the other did. Chris was quite happy to accept Pat's pacifist attitude but that did not mean that he had to be like him or not disagree with him.

He had other people who thought like himself, and he would discuss plans and strategies with them of how they would get it through to the British that they were not wanted in Ireland and to put it politely to them that they should leave, preferably peacefully – or if not, then by force.

Many nights were spent with different friends going over plans, but at the time it was a bit like playing soldiers when they were younger. Did they really believe that war would come to pass? They spent time in the mountains and hills around Northern Ireland in the evenings, training.

It was like one of their childhood games but this one was for grown-ups. It was something that could happen and they had to be prepared. Chris was following in the footsteps of his Irish heroes in Irish history. He thought there was a possibility that he might, one day, have to put all he was learning into action, but didn't really believe it one-hundred percent. If it came to pass that he would have to fight for his country's freedom, then he would not be seen wanting.

At this time, he continued his education and dealt with everyday living. He went up and down to Donegal most weekends and spent every Easter, summer and Christmas there. He also spent as much time as he could with Colly and her grandmother. In his immediate circle, he felt that Colly was the only one who really listened to him about how the Northern Ireland situation was. She seemed to be able to see and understand everything that he was saying.

Their love of their country and its people and the need to hold onto their culture such as the language and the music played a big part in their lives. They spoke fluent Gaeilge, and both played Irish music and sang. They had their inherent belief that no other country had a right to think that they could own or control part of their homeland. This made them very close friends and gave them a strong, mutually supportive system as they grew into adulthood.

In most children, as they grow and mature into adults they forget their childhood dreams and go on to something else, but not so with Chris and Colly. They had become more intense about them. Even though they included more things in their life, their patriotism always played a major role.

Maybe if they had lost touch with each other over the years, which would have been quite natural with Chris being in Belfast a lot of the time, they might have changed or forgotten, but with them there was a closeness of spirit and understanding that was unusual. They could spend days by themselves and never get bored. They might not see each other for months and then when they did, it was like they had never been apart. They sometimes fought and argued but never about anything that was important. On all important issues, they agreed wholeheartedly.

The general opinion in the locality was that they would one day get married, but there was never anything sexual between them. When Chris was teased about Colly, he always had the same answer: "You can't marry your sister."

They never thought of each other in that way. Maybe they knew too much about each other; there was no mystery. If anyone teased either of them about going out together, they couldn't understand why they would think that way. They were best friends – that was all!

At one point, early on in their teens, they had tried to cuddle and hold hands, but it didn't seem right. Colly told Chris, "It is like doing something wrong with your brother."

Neither of them felt comfortable about it. Over the years, both of them had relationships with other people, and neither minded. There was no jealousy. As a matter of fact, Colly had often tried to match-make Chris with different girls she knew. These girls could never understand how Colly could be so close to a man and not have a deeper relationship with him than friendship. Colly couldn't understand why some of the girls couldn't have a platonic relationship with a man.

She once asked Chris, "Why do some girls always have to bonk the men they go out with?"

Chris told her it was the primitive instinct. She laughed.

Colly always said that if there was no sexual chemistry in a relationship, you cannot put it there by trying. As far as she was concerned, that was the end of that conversation.

They both carried on with life. Chris finished his education and got a job in an engineering firm in South Donegal. One part of his dream had come to fruition. He was now living permanently in the county he loved, and not far from Colly or his family.

Chapter Nine

After Colly had been on the two-day training session in the Leitrim Mountains, she took a few days to herself and did a lot of thinking. Reality had hit home. She knew the route she was on and where it was leading, and she had to make sure she was ready go further and that she was able for it. Now it was here and she had to make sure that she wanted to carry through with the plan. Once she agreed, there would be no turning back.

The deciding factor came later that week with a phone call telling her that Laura's son in Belfast, Ben, had been shot dead by the British Army during a riot. Colly screamed to heaven with anger, and then she packed her bags and headed to Belfast to be with Laura.

When she returned, she got in touch with Chris and told him that she wanted to speak to him and Pat O'Hagan; she had decided what she was going to do.

It had taken a lot of sleepless nights and a lot of talking to herself, but she had always known in her bones that if it came to this moment, she would have only one option. All her life had been heading in this direction even though she had never consciously admitted it. She knew she could trust both men she was throwing her lot in with, and she owed it to them to be honest with them.

She had worked out what she was prepared to do and how much of a risk she was prepared to take. She'd had to think of her family and their safety, and whether the three of them could pull off the plans they had.

She was going to do her bit for her country because she could not find it in herself not to. Her Nan would be proud of her, and she would look after her and protect her from above.

The three of them met in her house, and after some interesting debating between herself and Pat and a lot of swapping of insults, Chris had to call a truce between them. They finally got down to planning their campaign. There were some arguments about tactics and targets but eventually the plan was hatched.

Colly said that she could not go out and shoot someone face to face or even from a distance. Apart from the fact that she did not think she was a good enough markswoman, she knew she would not be able to bring herself to pull the trigger to kill another person – not even British soldiers whom she hated with a vengeance. But she was quite prepared and willing to leave bombs in buildings and businesses, with the proviso that adequate warning would be given to clear the buildings of everyone.

She had decided that the best way to really get rid of the Brits was to hit them where it really hurt – in the pocket. The more buildings they had to replace and the more people they had to compensate, the more it was going to cost them to stay in Ireland.

It was decided the men would go after the security forces in their campaign. As far as the three of them were concerned, they were legitimate targets. They were targets of war no matter how many times the British said it wasn't a war. The Republican movement knew they had declared war on Bloody Sunday. Their army was trained for war and they had brought it to Northern Ireland, and if war was what they wanted, then war was what they were going to get. They had no right to be in Ireland and the sooner they left, the sooner the Troubles would be over.

The three of them had to work out all the details including protecting their identities, making sure that none of them would become suspects and that none of their families would be put in danger. Pat and Chris decided to pull back from their other involvements with the IRA and would keep a low profile. There was a lot of work to do.

They also spoke of taking in a fourth person. They felt they needed someone who knew the countryside and could find places where they could keep up their training without putting themselves in danger. They didn't want to speak to any of the guys in the IRA because the less who knew about what they were doing, the better.

At the end of the night, after many ideas had been tossed back and forth, Chris said, "I believe we have just declared war on the British, and from this day forth, we must never let anyone suspect what we are doing. We must guard our own and each other's lives and identities. No one outside of ourselves must know of anything we do or say."

With this, they made a sacred pact to protect each other.

It wasn't long after this that they heard about the mystery of the missing arms lost by the Unionists. They found it amazing and very funny that a whole stash of arms could disappear and that no one had a clue what had happened.

Chris decided he would do a bit of investigating and Pat said he would help. Pat had been on different trips in the area of the disappearance with units, and he said he would ask around to see if any of the IRA knew anything. Chris knew a few "good men" who lived in that area that he could talk to. After a while, they started to whittle down the suspects to a couple of men. After asking around, they discovered that one of the men had been ill at the time of the disappearance, so that only left Tom.

This was when Chris decided to pay Tom a visit, and a few days later he met him in the woods by the sea on that fateful evening. Tom joined their group within a week of their meeting and the four of them began their association which was to last for over twenty years.

Chapter Ten

It was a very wet evening and Colly was in Belfast, setting up business courses, when she got a call from Pat telling her that he and Chris were collecting a box of detonators from a house in a little town on the Tyrone border. She decided to meet them and take what she needed, and they could conceal the rest in a safe place until they were needed again.

She had become an expert at making bombs and now liked to do all her own work on them.

"If anything goes wrong," she said, "I only have myself to blame."

But she was too methodical to leave anything to chance. She had spent a lot of time over the years in some of the best bomb-making schools in the world. She had been to Libya, Syria and America, and had worked with some of the best experts in the business. Since her children had grown up and she was her own boss, she could do what she wanted when she wanted. Most of her waking hours were taken up with The Troubles. If her friends knew what she was doing when she was supposed to be sunbathing in the Grand Canaries, they would be astounded.

No! Colly left nothing to chance and never expected anyone to do anything that she wouldn't do herself. As the years went by, it just became another part of her life. A very important part, but nevertheless just something she did in her part in fighting the war for freedom.

Many times she wondered how she had ended up as she did, especially when she was on a job and the fear was churning her stomach and the sweat was running down her back in terror. She often felt she would never be able to breathe normally again when she was walking in to a building to plant a bomb. Still, she continued.

On the evening in question, she had just come into the little town in Tyrone and was driving up the street when she saw the men. She drove on to turn to go back to them when she realised that an RUC man was walking towards them. She pulled in to the side of the road and got out of the car. She turned and started to walk after the policeman, leaving about twenty yards between them. As she said afterwards, she had a bad feeling about it.

She saw him stop to watch Chris in the car and turn as Pat came out of the house and then she saw him reach for something inside his coat. She didn't stop to think. Obviously he had seen something that he thought was suspicious. She didn't know at that time what it was, but as far as she was concerned, he was not going to shoot Chris or Pat as long as she could help it. She walked rapidly towards him. She didn't run, which afterwards she found amazing, but she reached the policeman in seconds.

She reached into her shoulder bag and took out her handgun, which she had taken to carrying a few years before, and walked up behind the RUC man. As she did, she could see his revolver in his hand. She pushed her gun into his back and told him, "Walk back the way you have come from, and don't turn around to look at me or you're a dead man!"

It was getting dark and it was still raining, and she prayed that he would do as he was told. She found herself feeling very calm.

She brought him sideways onto her car, opened the boot and told him to get in. He went in very quietly. She was surprised at how quietly. She closed the lid of the boot after she had taken his gun and radio from him. She then told him through the lid that he would not be hurt if he did what he was told, and would get home safe if he made no fuss.

She said quietly to him, "I'm sure you realise that I will have to shoot you if you cause trouble, and remember now, the less you see, the less likely you are to be shot in the future. So get your priorities right – your life or your job."

She drove back to Pat and Chris and said, "Get the hell out of here now. I'll explain later."

She ran back to her car and drove out on the road. The realisation came to her at what she had done and the situation she was in. She kept driving for a few miles trying to decide what to do. What really bothered her was whether the policeman had time to radio in his suspicions and whether she was going to run into a checkpoint. She decided she would have to stop soon and let him out, she couldn't risk going much further with him in the boot in case she was stopped.

She pulled in to the side of the road and got out of the car. She knocked on the boot lid, and once again spoke to her captive.

"Can you hear me?" she said.

"Yes!" came back the answer.

"Now I am going to tell you what to do, and remember I have a gun trained on you, and believe me, I definitely know how to use it. I will open the boot lid and you will keep your head down and not look at me. You will step out of the boot, still with your head down, and go to the grass verge and lie down. I know it's wet, but better to be a little wet than dead. Do I make myself clear?"

"Yes!" came back the answer again.

"Now I want no heroics, which I'll be waiting for. Just do as you're told and both of us will be safe," she said.

"Now, get out of the boot backwards," she said as she opened it up. "Don't lift your head when I drive away. I'll be looking in the rear-view mirror and if you do, I will come back and blow it off you. Remember, I have your gun and I'm sure you'd hate to be shot with it."

"I promise you I'm no hero. I've just discovered that in this boot," replied the policeman.

He did as he was told. She got back into the car, drove off and watched in the mirror. The man definitely had got his priorities right, he kept his head well down on to his arms and never moved until she was gone from sight.

She had driven off in the opposite direction to home and after a few miles, doubled back along another road and arrived home in just over an hour. She was sweating and shaking by this time. She found it very hard to get the key in the door – her hands were shaking so much she had to hold it with both hands. When she reached the sitting room, she collapsed onto the couch. It was quite a few minutes before her breathing returned to normal.

Then it finally hit her what she had done. She could have been killed. She could have been in jail by now. This was the first time she had come face to face with a live target, and the shock was setting in.

"Bloody hell, woman! You have some guts," she laughed to herself.

She turned on the radio to hear the news, but there was nothing about the incident on it. Maybe the police were hushing it up. Maybe they did not want to let the public know that a woman had kidnapped one of them, put him into the boot of her car, left him in the middle of the country and stole his gun and radio, and had got away with it.

Oh! Bloody hell! The gun and radio were still in her car. She ran to the phone and rang Chris.

"Can you get over here now? I need to talk to you urgently."

"Are you OK?" he asked.

"Hopefully I will be, but get over here now, and bring Pat with you," she replied.

When they arrived and heard what she had done, they could not believe she'd had the nerve to pull it off, and more to the point, she had seemingly got away with it. They were in two minds whether to believe her or not until they saw the gun and radio.

"Will you take these and lose them somewhere or stash them until later? They may come in handy at a later date," she said.

"We'd better smash the radio and dump it. They might be able to trace the signal," said Pat.

They discussed what she had done and questioned her on the reaction of the RUC man. After a while Pat said, "What have we got on our hands, Chris?"

"A holy terror, from the looks of things," Chris laughed. "Colly! Do you realise what you have got away with? You could have been killed."

"Don't tell me," Colly replied. "I'm just realising myself what I have done, and I think shock has set in. I need a drink."

"Get her a brandy, Chris," said Pat, "and get me one too. I think we all need a drink after this. I'll look after the radio and gun. Tom will know what to do with them. He always said you were a brave cutty and now I have no doubts about it."

Pat had one drink with them and left to find Tom. Afterwards, he returned and they talked and drank into the night, discussing why the policeman had become suspicious, amongst other things. None of them could come up with an answer and it wasn't until a few weeks later that the mystery was solved.

It seemed that the "safe" house they had collected the detonators from was under suspicion by the RUC, and when the policeman had seen the car stopped outside it and then Pat coming out carrying a box, he had put two and two together and decided to play the hero. If he hadn't decided he could handle it himself and called for reinforcements first, then both Chris and Pat would have been caught and by now would be in Castlereagh or some other interrogation centre. Luck had definitely been on their side that night.

This was a very sobering thought to the three comrades and they decided to check more diligently in future on their safe houses before they went in to an operation.

Colly often thought afterwards about what the repercussions would have been if luck had gone against them. She wondered what her parents would have said, or the effect it would have had on her children.

Her mum had listened to all the same stories her mother had told her, and Colly could not understand why they didn't affect her in the same way they had affected her. Was it the usual rebellion against how your parents felt? Had her mother been too close to it all? Did it have to miss a generation for the next generation to see the problems and the cause of them, and have the realisation that it was up to them to look for a solution?

Colly could not understand why all Irish people would not come out and demonstrate en masse against the invasion in Northern Ireland. If they did, then there would be no need for bombing and bloodshed.

When the Government brought in the law banning all Irish Republican songs and all Irish people with Republican or Nationalist tendencies from being broadcast, Colly believed that a lot of Irish people's pride in their culture and heritage had been undermined. People who before had been proud of their culture now became ashamed, and Republicanism became a dirty word and Nationalism went under the table, only to be spoken about in private.

This made Colly very angry, firstly at the Irish government and the

Broadcasting Authority for implementing this rule, and secondly at the Irish people for letting them.

Why, she thought, *should we be ashamed of our history? It wasn't us who invaded another country and terrorised its people. Why couldn't they see the right and wrong of it? We are not a stupid people. Look at what we have achieved down through the ages against all the oppression. We have a great educational system, great playwrights, brilliant stars in sports, music, film and theatre, and against all the odds, the country with the greatest sense of humour in the world. Maybe it really was the only open air asylum in the world. Maybe we were all crazy. Well! If we are, we found our way of being so.*

She worried about her children and the impact her activities could have on them. They were bigger now and very sensible young people, but it would be a terrible shock to them if they were to discover what their mother was up to.

To have their mother in jail for involvement in terrorist activities, as the media calls it, would certainly not endear her to them, she thought.

Although she thought this, it did not change her way of thinking. She believed what she was doing was right.

Life continued like this for them all. They carried out operations, each in their own way. The only real change was that they became a lot more careful.

Colly would watch the news on the television and see another building flattened or another shooting incident that her unit was involved in. She would listen to the debates and sometimes she would see a glimmer of hope for a solution to it all. Then something else would happen to dim, and finally extinguish, that hope.

She listened to Maggie Thatcher. How she hated that woman! As far as Colly was concerned, the woman had no humanity. All her arrogance and her fight for power made her nothing but an unfeeling machine. She, as far as Colly was concerned, could have finished the whole conflict in Ireland if her arrogance had not got in the way.

History will prove that, thought Colly, *she should have given in to the few demands of the hunger strikers, but no, she had to show her power. And what had that done but caused more bloodshed? She had also created more Irish martyrs and recruited a bigger army for the*

IRA. The stupid woman, she should have realised how the Irish thought; now we are going to have to continue to show her.

John Major was no better, just in a more useless way, and as Tom once called him, "A didderer. Completely ineffectual."

A lot of things were happening in Colly's life at that time. Her children were getting older and were finishing school. Two of them were already working, with the other two finishing their education. Her eldest girl had finished an advanced course in Business Studies and Computers and wanted to be involved in her mother's business. This was natural, but if she travelled with her, Colly could not remain actively involved in the campaign. She was keeping her in the office for the time being and encouraging her to develop her own contacts.

No matter what she herself was involved in, she had decided early on that she would not try to influence her children one way or another. They all knew her stand on the Troubles and sometimes she had to bite her tongue to stop herself saying more than she should when they were debating the Troubles. She left them to make up their own minds, in the same way that she had.

Over the years, they had heard all the stories her Nan had told her.

"No one made me do what I am doing, so I don't see why I should expect anyone else to become involved," she had told Tom, Chris and Pat, and they had agreed with her.

She was relieved really that none of her children showed any inclination to follow in her footsteps. She loved them too much and would worry herself sick if she thought that one of them was active in the struggle.

She had a great relationship with them. They went on holidays every year together. She had shown them most of Ireland. They went camping, climbed mountains and found secluded beaches and swam. They stayed in hostels and caravans, and talked incessantly. It didn't matter what the subject was, they could have a heated debate about anything.

As her children got older and her business was pretty well-established – she had three people working for her now plus her daughter – things started to get easier for Colly. She had the house that her Nan had left her, she was financially secure, the kids didn't seem to need her anymore and she had more time on her hands. When she looked back on it, she could see that it was around this time that her thinking started to change.

She started to question their methods and search for another solution.

Reasonable people would sit down and work out their problems. But there is nothing reasonable about the British, she often thought. Even today they cannot see that we are not the hick bog men and women that they thought us to be.

She thought, *Maybe I'm getting lazy? Maybe life is becoming too easy and I don't want to put in the effort anymore?*

But she knew this wasn't it. The world was changing and so was people's thinking. The European Economic Community was changing everyone's perspective. No longer was the British oppression going to be tolerated in the modern world. There had to be another way besides the bomb and the bullet. People had to start talking, and that meant they would have to speak to people they did not want to speak to. A compromise had to be sought and found.

"Dear God! We'll never get Tom to come around to that way of thinking," said Colly to Chris and Pat when they would discuss it.

"All we can do is try," they argued. "We have to look at other alternatives. We would be burying our heads in the sand if we didn't."

There was another reason why Colly wanted it all to end – she was scared for the others. She had eased off a lot in her active involvement and the men understood this. They would never dispute the fact that she had done her share. But they were still involved in running their part of the campaign as much as ever. She felt that their luck couldn't hold out forever. Up until now, they had got away scot-free. There had been many close shaves, but they had always got home safe.

She had the utmost respect for Tom but she loved Chris and Pat. Just as much as each other, but in a different way.

After Colly's first training session with Pat, when she discovered that he was the commander, she really resented him. When she thought of what she felt was his underhand deceit, patronising attitude and arrogance, she couldn't even think of him without getting mad.

Who the hell did he think he was, she thought, *bloody Michael Collins?*

For ages afterwards, Chris had a real problem trying to cool her down. At every opportunity when she met him, she would rant and rave about Pat. Chris couldn't understand this at all. He knew Colly never went overboard with her emotions, and this reaction to Pat was puzzling.

He tried to talk to her about him. He told her how he was the best soldier the IRA had ever had, and how he was accepted and respected in all Republican circles. No matter where he went, people liked him. And he told her that when Pat was on the training courses, he was only doing his job, and that if he didn't do it right, then it was your neck that might be on the line next time.

None of this seemed to get through to her. She had a problem reasoning with all of this. She would hold long conversations with herself at how she was overreacting. She eventually cooled down enough to tell Chris that she realised that Pat was good at what he did and that he would be an asset in their unit, but that did not mean that she had to like him.

Chris couldn't understand her. All her life she had been sensible, level-headed. Now for some reason, she had decided to act totally illogically, and for no good reason other than the fact that he and Pat had taken a hand at her by not telling her who the commander was that first day. And if that was the case, why was she not as mad at him? He couldn't understand it and it worried him.

One evening, Pat and Chris arrived at her door, completely unexpected. Chris had decided not to give her time to work herself up into a temper. When she opened the door, Colly was so surprised to see them. She thought that Chris was still in Belfast, where he had gone the week before. She just let them in without comment and put the kettle on for tea.

If nothing else, Pat was a good talker and before she started on him, he decided to get his say in.

"Look, Colly, I know you don't like me. That's fine, you're entitled to your opinion. But what we have to think of now is what the best way for us to go forward with our plan is, and forget about our personal differences. If you believe in what you want to do, then you will see that I'm right. I will stay as much out of your way as I can and we won't have to meet each other apart from the work we will be doing together or for strategy planning. Can you agree with this?" he asked.

As Colly later said to Chris, "Unless I was an idiot, what else could I do but agree? After all, he was right. I had to put the good of the country before my own feelings."

But on the night, Colly's feelings were far from settled. She knew what he was saying was true. She had to try and work with him, and they needed him if they were to be an effective unit. But all she could think was, *Look at him, he's like a blooming tailor's dummy!*

Pat sat there six feet tall, dark-haired, tanned, good looking, and dressed in a brown suede jacket, cream shirt and beige trousers. She almost snorted at him when she looked at him. He seemed so perfect. He hadn't a hair out of place and his shoes practically gleamed. She just could not equate the man she had met on the training session in the middle of a Leitrim mountain with this model of perfection. She thought she preferred the other man on the mountain, rough and loud as he was. This man looked as though he had stepped out of a magazine, the type who is supposed to appeal to all women.

"But not to me!" snorted Colly.

She couldn't understand why she had taken such an aversion towards him. He really hadn't done anything terrible to make her feel like this.

Well, nothing more than Chris had done, she thought.

They had a little fun at her expense, but she had been made fun of before and she could certainly deal with being taken a hand at. She had a very good sense of humour. As a matter of fact, she was known to have suffered a lot of fools gladly, sometimes even way beyond a normal person's point of endurance, and made allowances for them.

With Pat it was completely different. She continually argued with him on any point she disagreed with. She would very seldom give in. After a while, their arguments practically became notorious. Chris often left them still arguing, and told them that when they came to a decision, to let him know and he would go along with them. Luckily, he trusted both of them and knew that when they finally agreed, it would be a reasonable and practicable decision. He knew that they would eventually see sense and that this was just a hiccup that they were going through. Often their arguments were over points of law or politics. It was never over anything that would jeopardise the unit or a specific operation.

After her initial antagonism, Colly knew that Pat was an astute and intelligent operator. She listened to how he felt their unit should be run and quickly realised that their thinking was very much the same. They had decided that Pat would be their contact with other units in the country and that none of their names would be divulged to anyone else. The unit was to be as secret as possible, and this, they felt, was the only way to guarantee their success and safety.

It was also Pat that devised the plan for Colly's briefcase. He spent hours in her workshop out the back and wanted something she could carry that wouldn't bring attention to her. He hit on the plan of the briefcase because of her work. She dressed in suits mainly for her work, and what would be more natural than for her to carry a briefcase?

When he had the prototype finished and showed it to her, she was amazed. It looked just like any ordinary briefcase except maybe a little broader. There was a space running up the centre to hold a rectangular metal box. The actual case itself was metal, covered with leatherette. Four plates at the bottom held in the metal container and when you pressed a lever on the handle, they slid back so that when you lifted the briefcase off the floor, you left the container behind.

They then got an associate of Pat's to mass produce the metal boxes to specific measurements so that there were compartments in them to hold the detonator, timing device and the explosives.

Colly could walk in to any building, look around her, find a suitable location for the bomb, put her briefcase on the floor, press the lever, pick up her case and walk out the door, leaving the bomb behind her. She had come in with a briefcase and had left with a briefcase. Who was to know any different?

She became so engrossed in camouflaging the bombs. She would visit the buildings some time before she would plant the bomb and work out a colour scheme to make them less detectable. She wanted to make sure that they couldn't be seen as soon as she left.

She became quite the artist, painting the boxes in different colours to fit in with the surrounding décor, using ordinary paint which was mass produced. When she returned, she would leave it beside a flower display, ornament, wall or statue. The others used to laugh at her, but her plan worked and she was never detected.

Job satisfaction to her was when she did as much damage as possible to the building without anybody getting hurt. When she planted the bomb, she would then ring Pat or Chris who would ring in the warning to clear the building. This covered her in every way. It was a man's voice who rang in the warning with a Northern Ireland accent, which they had; no one was injured and she just walked away free.

Another area which Colly became an expert in was masking her identity. When she did the reconnaissance of the building, she wore one wig, and when she delivered the bomb, she wore another. By just changing her hairstyle and make-up, she could change her whole appearance. Scraping back her hair, gelling it and putting it in a bun with a hairnet over it made it look darker. Pencilling her eyebrows, wearing darker foundation, shading her cheekbones and wearing a darker lipstick changed the whole look of her face. Change the style of outfit along with this, and you had a different woman.

This part Colly enjoyed. She had about three different wardrobes of clothes, half a dozen wigs and dozens of pairs of shoes. Most of these she bought in second-hand shops. She also made a very distinguished older woman.

After a short while, she became so good at disguising herself that she often fooled Pat and Chris. On one occasion, she spent some minutes talking to Tom in a pub. He didn't recognise her, and she eventually had to give in and tell him who she was because he thought she was chatting him up and he was trying to get away from her to go to meet Pat and Chris, which Colly knew about, and she couldn't keep from laughing.

Her wigs and costumes led to one of Colly's scariest moments with the security forces. She had been stopped at a checkpoint on her way to Belfast, and instead of being waved on as usual, she was asked to step out of the car. This was the first time it had happened to her.

The soldier looked in her case in the boot and saw her wigs, and asked what they were for. She told him she was an amateur actress on her way to taking part in a play in Belfast. He then came to the front of the car and looked at her briefcase on the floor, the one with the bomb in it, and asked her what she had in it. She said scripts and other computer work.

"Oh God!" she begged silently. "Don't let him ask me to open it. He will never understand the centre being a steel box."

The next thing she heard was a voice behind them shouting, "Come on, boys, you've seen her legs and anything else you wanted to see by now. Get on with it!"

She could see the anger in the soldier's eyes. She smiled and said, "He's a very ignorant person, isn't he?"

"Oh! We know how to deal with his kind, which he is just going to learn now. On you go. Break a leg."

The last thing she saw in the rear-view mirror was the soldiers taking the man out of the car and putting him up against it, spread-eagled. She didn't know who he was but she could have kissed him.

Oh boy, she thought. *I was born to live another day.*

Before she returned, she decided to get herself another briefcase and leave the other one behind her in Belfast with a friend. She could collect it later. Sure enough, as she returned through the checkpoint, her car was searched and her briefcase examined. They were a new regiment and were doing a thorough job. They usually did when they first arrived, but as they got to know you, after a while they would wave you on.

When she got through she smiled and thought, *Yeah! There is someone up there on my side. Thanks, Nan!*

Chapter Eleven

Life continued like this. Colly did her thing and the men did theirs. They were very seldom seen in public together. They generally met in her house if they had to, but the men devised their own plans together sometimes weeks before an operation, or even months if a specific event was being targeted. Either Chris or Pat would fill her in on what was happening.

She and Chris still went out socially in the locality; people expected this and passed no remarks.

They were a good team and there were very few disagreements between them. Tom had found his niche in life and something to live for, and had made a few good friends in them. He adored Colly and she had the greatest respect for him. If she told him to jump off the bridge, he would have done it. He admired her bravery and had put her on a pedestal as one of his greatest heroines. It was probably that she made the time to talk to him whenever they met and was so down to earth that made him admire her so much.

Colly and Pat continued with their arguing for quite a while, but eventually it died a natural death due to their mutual respect for each other. They knew that the work they were doing was too important to continue bickering. When it came to planning an operation, there was agreement all around unless someone had serious misgivings about something.

Things would have continued like this if Colly had not decided to go on holiday with her children. All of them were very energetic people and into physical activities in a big way. She spent the most active holiday with them that she could remember. They went horse riding, swimming, snorkelling, climbing and just walking. She felt exhilarated when they arrived home.

As they pulled into her driveway, Pat arrived.

"Where the hell have you been?" he shouted at her. "I thought you were supposed to be gone a fortnight."

"What the hell is wrong with you?" she asked. "I've only been gone a fortnight; has something happened?"

"You were nearly three weeks away," said Pat.

"Actually, I was two weeks and one day gone, and I told you that was how long I was going to be when I left," she answered. "What is wrong with you? Are Chris and Tom alright?"

"Yes," he replied.

"Well! What is wrong?" She looked at him, puzzled.

"Nothing," he answered. "I was just worried when I didn't hear from you."

And he turned and walked away.

What is up with that man, she thought. She then smiled to herself, *At least he was worried. I suppose I should have rang. What did he think would happen to me with the kids with me? They could look after me, never mind me looking after them.*

But she was surprised at herself at how pleased she was about the fact that he was worried about her.

After that evening, she didn't see him for about a week. Chris rang her a few times to tell her that he was worried about him as he was acting completely out of character and taking the heads off people without any good reason. Colly told him that he would be alright and that he'd get over whatever was bothering him.

"You don't understand, Colly," said Chris. "When I speak to him sometimes, he doesn't hear me. I think there is something serious worrying him. Have you any idea what it could be? When I asked him if he had spoken to you since you came back he said, "Yeah! I bloody did. Why?" and he looked at me strangely. Did you two have a fight?"

"No," said Colly.

She told him what had happened on the evening she came back from holidays.

"Ho! Ho!" said Chris. "I think I know now what's wrong."

"Well! Would you mind enlightening me as to why he took the head off me?" replied Colly.

"Oh! I'm sure you'll find out in time. Pat's a sensible guy and he will eventually see sense, and then I'm sure he will tell you himself. I'll see you at the weekend. Bye."

Damn him, thought Colly. *It's not my fault if Pat is doing a moody, and I'm not going to worry about it.*

But she did worry and she was surprised at how she missed hearing from him. He had taken to phoning her once or twice a week, just for a chat, and now he had stopped since she had come home and had the run-in with him. She thought about phoning him but something always stopped her. She was afraid she might hear something she didn't want to.

All that week was spent waiting to hear from him. Lying in bed at night, she wondered what could be wrong. Sleep just wouldn't come and every night she tossed and turned. The worry of him not getting in touch was affecting her badly. He had always rung, once or twice a week, since they had called a truce a few years before. She was used to having him in her life and missed him.

No word came from him until the following week. Finally, he rang one evening at about ten o'clock and sounded very subdued.

"I need to talk to you," he said. "It's important."

"OK," she answered quietly. "I'll be here all day tomorrow by myself. The kids are all away."

"I'll see you sometime in the afternoon then," he replied and rang off.

She did not ask any questions and afterwards, she found that she was shaking and could not understand why. The urge to talk to him was great, and on the other hand, the fear of what he might say was greater. She was totally confused about her feelings. She just could not think straight. What was going on in her head? It was totally mixed up.

At the crack of dawn the next day, she was up and pacing the floor or scrubbing the house. Keeping herself busy seemed to be the only solution.

"It's only Pat and we've been friends for years," she kept saying. "Why am I so worried about meeting him?"

Every nook and cranny was scrubbed by ten o'clock. Then she showered and changed. Getting dressed was another dilemma. What would she wear? It didn't help that there were three wardrobes of clothes to choose from.

Should it be jeans and a shirt or a skirt, maybe that was too casual; maybe a dress – no, that was not what she wore at home and he knew this. She eventually gave up and put on her blue jeans and a white T-shirt.

He arrived just after twelve.

Her nerves were shattered by this time. There was almost a hole worn in the sitting room carpet with her pacing when she heard him pull into the driveway. Going to the window, she watched him get out of the car and walk towards the house. The thought of how she used to criticise him for his dress sense and his "band box" appearance crossed her mind. Now she realised with shock that he was everything she wanted and that his appearance was the dearest sight she could imagine. The worried look on his face as he walked towards her made her heart go out to him.

She went to the door to meet him. He looked at her.

"Hi," he said quietly.

She smiled at him and they stood looking at each other for a few moments. She reached up her hand and touched his face.

"Hi, yourself," she smiled.

He looked at her and smiled. It was as though they could read each other's minds. He put out his arms and she stepped into them.

"Oh thank God," she heard him whisper as he held her.

"Why?" she asked.

"I was so worried that you would not want to know how I felt about you," he said. "I love you, you know?"

"Yes, I know now," she answered. "And I love you too."

"I missed you when you were away and I couldn't stop thinking about you. Every day I would go to the phone to call you, and then I would realise that I couldn't get in touch because you were on holidays. After a few days, I began to go crazy and I knew then how much you meant to me and that I didn't ever want to be without you again. That really shocked me!"

"Oh yes!" smiled Colly. "And why was that?"

"We've been friends for so long now and it never occurred to me that I was in love with you. I can't understand why because I now know that I have been for many years," answered Pat very seriously.

"Yes!" said Colly. "I just discovered about two minutes ago how I really feel about you when I saw you walking towards me from your car. I also know why I was feeling so confused about all the feelings I've been experiencing this week when you didn't ring."

They walked into the house, wrapped in the other's arms. Stopping, they looked at each other as though for the very first time. Then, they kissed with a fervour that sealed their unspoken promise to never again be parted. Slowly, Pat undressed Colly with a love and tenderness that spoke volumes, and they made love for the first time on the floor of the sitting room. Gently, they told each other how they felt, and a deluge of love poured from them.

Afterwards, Pat said as he held Colly, "I feel as though I have finally come home and I am really at peace, at last."

Outside, the sun shone and the birds sang, and all was right with the world for that short time.

Afterwards Colly mused, "I feel as though all the pieces in my life have come together and fit very nicely, and that fate has dealt a very nice hand to me today. What I can't understand is why we have not seen that this is how we felt about each other years ago?"

"Maybe it wasn't the right time until now. It really doesn't matter as long as we know now what we have. We are very good friends and know each other so well that we have developed a very solid foundation now for going forward from here," he replied. "Colly! Don't let us regret what might have been; let's just be grateful for what we have now."

"Yes, darling, you are right. So, where do we go to from here?" smiled Colly.

"Anywhere you want, my darling," replied Pat. "Anywhere you want! We can get married or live together – anything – as long as we can be together. I don't ever want to be apart from you again." Then he held her tight and kissed her.

"Oh dear!" said Colly, a little shocked. "I never thought about marriage. To me, it's like a bad word. Maybe we could put off thinking along those lines for a while. You know that it wasn't great for me the first time round, although I'm not comparing you with my husband. I don't know two people more different. But if you go through an experience like that, it taints your feelings about the institution itself."

"Don't worry," soothed Pat as he held her. "Maybe we can think of it further down the line. I won't pressurise you into doing anything you don't want to do."

"As long as we are together, that's all that matters. I suppose we really should think about what we are going to do. I don't want you living in one place and me in another. Have you any suggestions? If at all possible, I would like to continue living here. I love this house and I prefer living in the country to the city. But what about your business?" asked Colly.

Pat had moved back to Belfast years before and he still had a practice in Dundalk which he attended once or twice a week.

"I think it's time to move out of Belfast. I can set up a business here. For the moment, I can commute between the two, as you are doing. We'll make our base here. I wouldn't want to live anywhere else but here with you. I love this house too and to me it represents all that you stand for – love, warmth, happiness and solid loyalty. I don't know why I feel like that about a house, but I have always felt safe and secure here," said Pat.

"That's not the house," said Colly, "that's my Nan, she looks after me."

"I'm sorry that I never knew her," said Pat. "Chris often speaks about her. She must have been quite a woman."

"She was, and even though you may not have gotten to know her, I believe that she knows you and approves. I always feel that she is looking after me," said Colly.

"Well!" laughed Pat. "I hope that she continues to, and would you ask her to take me under her wing too?"

Afterwards, when they had dressed and were having something to eat in the kitchen, Colly started to giggle. Pat looked at her and smiled, "Come on, out with it, what are you thinking of now?"

"I know why I was so antagonistic towards you when I first met you. I knew you could be a danger to me and capable of hurting me if I fell in love with you," she answered half-jokingly.

Pat looked at her very seriously, and reached for and held her hand. "Believe me, Colly, I promise with all my heart that I will try not to hurt you in any way, and I will love and protect you as much as is humanly possible, in all that we do," he said.

"I believe that now," she replied. "I also know, respect and admire you. I believe that you are not capable of hurting someone you really care for and I know without a doubt, for some reason, that you love me as much as I love you."

Pat looked into her eyes very intently and answered, "Always remember that, my darling." Then he laughed, "Come over here and let me show you how very dangerous I really am." He grabbed her and said, "Let this dangerous man have his wicked way with you," and they proceeded to make passionate love again.

Later that weekend, Colly rang Chris.

"Pat and I want to talk to you," she said.

"Where is he?" replied Chris.

"He's with me at the house. Are you coming over?" she said.

"Oh! I wouldn't miss this for the world." Then he laughed, "I'll be there in a few minutes," and he put the phone down.

Colly stood puzzled, looking at the phone. "Is that man on drugs or am I missing something?" she mused.

When Chris arrived at the house, he looked from one to the other and laughed. "Well! Have you told each other that you're mad about each other?" he joked. "My guess is that you have, and if I may say so, it's about bloody time. I thought you were never going to get around to it."

They stood looking at him, astounded.

"How the hell did you know!?" they said in unison.

"It might have something to do with the fact that you, Pat, spent every free minute you had down here with Colly, on the pretext that you were devising some plan for her equipment. Or if she was on a job you were worried sick until she rang and said she was OK, or it might have been that you were always on the phone to each other or that you never stopped talking about each other," he laughed.

"We didn't," they said.

"Oh yes, you did!" Chris replied, laughing. "Me and Tom have wondered for years if you were ever going to recognise the fact yourselves."

"Tom knew too?" they asked, shocked. "Why did you never say anything?"

"We thought you would eventually get around to realising it yourselves," he laughed. "Well! Are we going to get a big day out of you two now?"

"We haven't decided yet," laughed Colly.

"Bloody hell," laughed Chris, "are we going to have to wait another twenty years before you decide to make a complete commitment to each other? Seriously though, I don't know any other two people who are more suited than you two are."

"You are only looking for a big day out as an excuse for getting drunk, and of course, to be my best man. Me and Colly know that we are committed to each other for the rest of our lives, and we don't need a piece of paper to prove that to anyone – not even to you," laughed Pat.

"Talking about getting drunk," said Chris, "where's the champagne?"

"We drank the only bottle we had last night, but I suppose you'd better get another one or we'll never hear the end of it. And you'd better ring Tom and get him to come over too, seeing as the two of you could see this coming, and we dare not leave one of you out. We can all celebrate together," laughed Colly.

When Chris left to get the drink and collect Tom, Colly and Pat discussed what Chris had just told them. They thought it was hilarious that the other two had realised what was happening between them, and they had not. They were more surprised that Chris had said nothing to either of them. It wasn't like him. Any excuse for a slagging match, and he usually never missed it.

Pat grew very serious, and Colly looked at him and said, "What is the matter, is something wrong?"

"No! But would you listen to me, just for a few minutes, without interrupting?" he asked, very seriously.

"Of course. Come on, Pat, you're scaring me," she said anxiously.

He got down on one knee and took her hand and said, "I know that you don't want to get married yet and I'm not going to push you into doing something you don't want to do. But I want to buy you a ring – call it an engagement ring, a commitment ring or whatever you like. I want to throw a party for all our close friends and relatives and let them know that we are committed to each other for the rest of our lives. What do you say?"

"I will have to talk to my children first before we tell anyone else, but yes! I would really like that," she replied. She then laughed, "Chris will have his excuse for a celebration now. I'm sure he'll be delighted!"

Pat kissed her and said, "You know we will be good together, don't you?"

"I've never been surer of anything else in my life," she replied. "I'm sure this is what fate had in store for us, and it is good."

They sat and held each other and spoke of their future together until Chris arrived back with Tom and the drink. Tom was just as glad as Chris about the news.

"This couldn't happen to a nicer couple," he said, "and the best of health and happiness to you both," and he toasted them.

The four of them sat and chatted for hours, and all of them felt at peace with the other. They had a very close bond, and Colly and Pat's commitment seemed to seal it tighter.

When Colly told her children about herself and Pat, their reaction was identical to the others. They had seen it coming all along and were very happy about the situation. They liked Pat and were glad that their mum was content. The fact that they were older and making their own way in life helped, and they didn't have to worry about her being on her own. Not that this was really an issue as they knew she was a very capable woman and not dependant on them. But it meant she had someone who loved her and whom she really loved with her when they weren't around.

A few weeks later they threw a big party. All their families and friends attended, and the feeling from everyone was of delight that the two of them had finally got together. They had got to know Pat over the years, and liked him.

Pat bought Colly a ring with an emerald in the centre and surrounded by diamonds. The emerald, they said, symbolised their love for Ireland, and the diamonds were their everlasting love for each other.

Tom's reaction when he saw the ring quite surprised Colly. She explained to him why they had picked that particular ring and he looked at it and said, "Now when I look at that ring, I'll tell you what I see. The emerald is Ireland alright, but the stones around it are all of us, with our friendship and love for Ireland, and each other, as solid as rocks. What do you think of that now?"

"You old romantic," laughed Colly and hugged him. "That's the first time I ever heard you being sentimental."

"I think a lot about what I have done over the years with all of your help, and the very good friends you have been to me. You have made my life very worthwhile, and if I hadn't met Chris when I did, I probably would have ended up a very lonely old man, going to the pub and never having any friends. If I never do anything else in my life from now on, I will know that I have done everything that I could for a cause I believed in, and that I have made three of the greatest friends any man could have in you and Chris and Pat," Tom answered in possibly the longest conversation on the subject that Colly had ever heard from him.

"Oh, go on," laughed Colly, "you must be drunk for you to talk so much."

"I may be, but always remember that a drunk person usually tells you what they really feel," he answered.

Chapter Twelve

After that conversation with Tom, Colly decided she would have to talk to him about looking at alternative ways to what they were doing, or leaving it to the politicians to work it out. Maybe if she came at it in a gradual manner, he would start to realise himself that they couldn't go on as they were. None of them were getting any younger and their thinking was changing, not only about their own group, but about others in the Republican movement.

When she spoke to the rest about this, they agreed, but didn't hold out much hope of changing Tom's mind. But anything was worth a try. They knew that he had decided how he wanted to achieve his goals a long time ago, and that he still believed it was the way to go.

His thinking process seemed to be that you set your goals and worked in a certain way towards them. No matter whose attitude or what circumstances changed, you kept going on your way because you believed it was right. If you changed your mind, didn't that mean you were wrong before, and if so, wasn't everything you did up to now wrong? From his way of working it out, this was not something he could live with.

How could he deal with the fact that what he thought was a just war, where he was the instigator of people being killed and injured, had not only been wrong, but that by just talking to the British, he would have achieved what he had set out to do originally – to get the British out of Ireland and get his country back for the Irish. No, Tom could not accept that.

When any of them tried to broach the subject with him, he dismissed it, and it was the same when Colly tried to speak to him. To Tom, Gerry Adams was a traitor because he had spoken to the British. He still thought that Martin McGuinness was a good man and that if he had his way, he said, he would tell McGuinness not to betray the others who had fought for their country.

"McGuinness was a man of the people, who knew what it was like to be out in the thick of it and he knew how the people felt. He wouldn't let Adams accept compromise, and the British government would know from McGuinness that they couldn't walk over the Irish like they had in the past," he repeated on numerous occasions.

Adams, to Tom, was a politician who was looking for glory, but as long as McGuinness was there, he would not get it at the price of betraying the Nationalist people.

When they argued that Adams was also a patriot, he just dismissed it.

When Colly looked back at Tom's life, she realised he was never going to change. When he decided not to go home after he had returned from America, he never changed his mind. That part of his life was over as far as he was concerned. His father had betrayed him by selling the farm. It didn't matter what his motives were or how noble he thought they were – he had let him down and Tom wanted no more to do with him. As far as his mother was concerned, she should have stopped his father. She should have known how much the farm meant to him, so that was her out of his life also. His brother and sister had never been very close to him so they didn't matter.

He never returned home again after that. The only contact he had with them was when he would send a Christmas card, which Colly would nag him into doing. His brother sometimes came to visit him, but he only stayed for a day or two. Colly often thought that it was only to find out if Tom was still alive.

Tom now lived about six miles from Colly in the middle of the countryside on a little farm which he had bought a few years before. He raised a few cattle, sheep and chickens, grew his own vegetables and saved his own hay and silage. The old car he drove had seen better days, as had his tractor. But he was quite content.

The house was very well looked after by him, as were his farmyard and byres. When he wasn't out on the farm working, which wasn't very often, or when he didn't have to go out on an operation with Pat and Chris, he spent his time reading. Mostly the books were on Irish history or on the history of other countries who had gained their independence from Britain. They seemed to impound in him the fact that the British should get the hiding of their lives before they left Ireland.

Colly, Pat or Chris would sometimes visit him. Each went individually at night so as not to draw attention to themselves. They were always very welcome, unless they brought up the subject of the peace talks. He would make the tea and put a drop of whiskey in it, "to keep out the cold," he would tell them, and they would chat for a while. The reaction was always the same if they tried to discuss other alternatives to a solution to the struggle. He would immediately change the subject and discuss the farm or the weather or anything else that came into his mind.

If you tried to insist, he would point out that the British had tricked and cheated on every agreement they had ever made with the Irish down through the ages. When it was pointed out to him that others were trying to talk to the British now and wanted another, more peaceful solution to the Troubles, he would say, "Let them, they're either traitors or idiots, and I'm not going to be either."

There was no getting through to him. After a while, they decided to give up on him. They knew he wouldn't change, and it worried them.

When Pat heard through the grapevine that the British had been in touch with the hierarchy of the IRA wanting to talk peace, he told Chris and Colly. They all prayed that this was the beginning of the end of their war. Perhaps this time, the English were serious and something might come out of it. They fervently hoped so.

They knew in their hearts that they had done all they could up to this point. They could not go on indefinitely with the same methods; it was not producing any significant results. And because their unit was a closed shop, no one else could be brought in to carry on their work. All that was possible for them to do had been done. They had fought as good a fight as any soldiers.

Now their aim was trying to stop the Unionists getting a stronghold on any arms or ammunition. Fear of them gaining any 'might' over the Nationalists in the North was all that prevented Chris and Pat from completely calling off all their activities.

Gradually, and almost imperceptibly, their activities grew less. No longer were they constantly looking for targets to attack.

Chris's life had developed a peace that he never remembered experiencing before. No longer was he plotting and planning. Nor was he always on the lookout to see what was happening in the

Loyalist camp. He also had developed his contacts over the years but now instead of gathering reconnaissance from them, he was looking forward to when he might one day meet them as friends.

He continued to run his engineering business which was doing well for him. There had been different women in his life but none of them had lasted very long. The girl he was going out with at that time was from Derry. He had met her through some friends of his one night at a dance, and they had hit it off right away. Of course, that may have come from the fact that her family were very involved in Republican activities.

She was an attractive brunette with brown eyes and a great personality. Their affair was now into its second year and had lasted longer than any of the others. Her name was Marie Connolly, and she was a few years younger than Chris. She was also the only girl that he had taken home with him. Colly hoped that he was now settling down, she felt that they suited each other very well and she really liked Marie. She would have hated it if he had become serious about someone she couldn't relate to.

"She's smart, and intelligent enough to keep manners on you," Colly laughed as she teased Chris.

When she joked with him about getting married, he always said that he was waiting for someone like her, only with the sexual attraction thrown in.

She would hit him and laugh and say, "Don't be daft, don't you know there is no one like me! You are just going to have to settle for second best. And remember, you are not getting any younger. Do you not want little Chrises running around calling you Daddy?"

At one point he got very serious.

"How could I expect any woman to share my life and have children with me when something could go wrong on one of our operations? I could get killed or jailed for twenty years. It would not be fair on her or the children," he said.

"I've done it," answered Colly. "You cannot always think of the worst scenario and go on living your life putting everything else on hold, in case something might happen."

"I haven't yet met someone who I feel would understand what I do and let me continue doing it. I couldn't expect anyone to," he replied seriously.

"Does Marie know what you are doing, and if not, don't you think she might understand? She does come from a very Republican background, you know. Most of her family are involved in the IRA!" said Colly.

"To tell you the truth, I've thought about it many times but I've always stopped myself," he replied.

"If you care about her and you know she cares about you, then I believe she has the right to be allowed to make the decision for herself. Even if you did tell her, what have you got to lose? She wouldn't grass on you, coming from the family she does. And you haven't been active for about six months now. Just don't tell her about the rest of the unit," said Colly.

"I'll think about it," he said.

Then he laughed, "Well! If I'm not going to find another you, she's probably the next best thing."

"Are you trying to tell me that you are serious about her?" teased Colly.

"Well, she's stuck around so far, and I haven't kicked her out of bed yet," he laughed. "Maybe I should think of making an honest woman of her."

"Oh Chris," said Colly. "I'm so glad. I'm sure that Marie will understand what you are doing when you tell her. She's a sensible girl and I'm sure she will accept what you do as part of the package. She's a very lucky girl to have you. What do you want to do, spend the rest of your life regretting what could have been if you only had the courage to open your mouth?"

"When you look at it that way, I believe you're probably right," he said. "You always were level-headed," he added, laughing.

When Chris left that evening, Colly wondered if he would tell Marie. If he did, would she accept him, and could she live with his way of life? She knew it was not going to be easy, especially when you loved someone. You were always expecting that phone call to tell you that they had been shot or jailed. Over the years, she had worried when the rest of the unit went out on a job. She never rested until she got that call that said they were safe.

She also knew what it was like to love someone and accept what they did, and try not to stop them. She often wished that Pat did not have to do what he did, that he would just sit behind his desk and attend court, and come home in the evening where she had the tea ready. She knew that this was not the kind of people they were, but nevertheless she worried and did not know what she would do if anything happened to him, or how she would live without him. She knew that Pat felt the same about her.

It was strange that while she was on a mission herself, she never worried. She had a very fatalistic approach to it. This, as far as she was concerned, was her mission in life. She knew the risks and took every precaution to minimise them. The rest was up to fate. She could never have done it if she had looked at it differently.

If she had worried about what her parents would think if they found out, or what her children would do without her if anything happened – whether it was getting herself killed or jailed – she could not have carried on. Her belief in what she was doing was ingrained in her. This belief would always have made her get involved in the fight for freedom, one way or another, so there was no point in worrying about it.

How, she thought, *could you expect someone else to fight your battle if you wouldn't do it yourself?*

Years ago, she had made her decision and she had followed it through. It was the same with the others. They believed that they had been right, up until now. But now they had to move on and find other solutions to end the conflict. They would follow any avenue open to them to achieve this. Their only worry was whether Tom would come along with them.

Chapter Thirteen

A few weeks after Colly had spoken to Chris, she was sitting at home, completing her work in the office. That week had been more strenuous than usual, and now a restless urge came over her to go for a long walk. There was nothing she loved more than strolling along the countryside with the sun shining down on her, listening to the birds and smelling the wild flowers and plants. She felt she needed the fresh air and a bit of exercise. The sun was high in the sky and the birds were singing as she ambled along beside the sea. She felt at peace with the world.

Pat had gone to Belfast during the week and would return that evening, and she couldn't wait to see him. Their relationship just seemed to carry on improving with the passing of time. With all relationships, there is bound to be some trepidation on both sides at the beginning at how things are going to work out. Miraculously, as far as she was concerned, living with each other was much more fulfilling than they could have ever hoped for.

She walked on with a smile on her face, deep in thought of Pat. After a few miles, she saw a car coming towards her and realised it was Marie's. As it passed, she waved and a few yards further on, the car pulled up. Colly turned to see Marie getting out of the car.

"Can I walk with you for a bit?" shouted Marie.

"Sure," said Colly as she walked towards her. "I'll be glad of the company. Are you coming from home?"

"No," she said, "I came down last night to stay with Chris, but I needed a while on my own to think, so I came out here to see you."

"Oh! Ho! That sounds ominous," joked Colly. "Can I help?"

"I hope so," Marie replied. "It's about Chris."

"Well! I'll try," laughed Colly. "Now what has he been up to?"

Marie looked at Colly very seriously.

"It's what he has been up to for years," she said. "He told me all about it during the week and he also told me that you know, so I know I'm not telling you anything that I shouldn't. But it's not about his involvement in the IRA that I want to talk to you about, I can live with that. If you come from Derry like I do and have a family like mine who have been involved in one way or another down through the years, you learn to live with it and accept it."

"So what's the problem then?" asked Colly gently.

"I don't really know how to put this," Marie replied. "I suppose I want to know what kind of a relationship you and Chris have or had. It bothers me because you are so close, and I don't want to step on someone's toes."

Colly started to laugh. "Oh, Marie! Is that all you're worried about? If I was a man and was Chris's friend, would you worry?" she asked.

"Of course not," Marie replied, "but that is different."

"To us it is pretty much the same!" said Colly. "Let me tell you how it is. I would say that Chris and I have the most platonic relationship that is possible between two people of different sexes. We tried to make something else out of it years ago but it felt a bit like I was kissing my brother. We have been friends since we were very young. We have been through our lives together as close as brother and sister. Don't you think that something would have come out of it by now if we had felt differently? He's my best friend, and I love and respect him. I think he's one of the greatest people I know, but that's it. I love Pat also but in a different way. I want to spend the rest of my life with him and I want him in my bed every night. If Chris was ever in my bedroom, it would only be to fix the heating. Is that what you wanted to know?"

Marie turned away for a few moments and when she turned back, she had a big grin on her face.

"That's what Chris told me when I asked him about you. After he proposed!" she said. "But I had to talk to you to find out if you felt the same."

"Marie! He proposed?" Colly was practically dancing on the road. "I'm so glad, you'll make a great couple," she said as she hugged Marie. "Come on, we must have a drink to celebrate; we'll go to the pub for one."

"Oh! I can't, and you mustn't let Chris know that I told you. He wants to tell you himself," said Marie worriedly.

"I won't tell him, but I'm so glad that he has told you everything and that he has asked you to marry him." Colly stopped for a moment, startled, and asked anxiously, "You *are* going to marry him?"

"Oh! I definitely am now," laughed Marie.

"Come on, we're going to the pub anyway. I could be doing with a drink after this. I'm so happy Chris is not going to be on his own for the rest of his life, and that there will be little Chrises and Maries running around," Colly laughed.

She tucked her arm into Marie's, and they walked back to the car, laughing.

When Chris arrived at Colly's house that evening with Marie to tell Colly and Pat the news, she acted all surprised, and hugged and kissed him. She looked at Marie over Chris's head and winked.

"Welcome to the gang, Marie," she said.

"Thanks, Colly," replied Marie. "I think I'm going to enjoy being around you lot, you are all a little bit mad!" she added, laughing.

"You could be right," laughed Pat. "I've thought it for a while myself. But I think it's more than a little bit!"

Colly wondered how long it would be before they would get married.

"If it takes him as long as it took him to pick a woman, we could be decrepit old bodies," she laughed to Pat. "And we'll all be going around on Zimmer frames!"

But later that week, she was in for a surprise. The phone rang on Wednesday night, and when she answered, Chris said to her, "Have you a decent dress to wear to a big occasion?"

"I suppose so," answered Colly. "Why? Where are we going?"

"Myself and Marie are getting married in two months' time in Derry," he replied.

"I don't believe it," laughed Colly. "So you really are going to take the plunge. Well done, my old friend, I'm so glad."

"I do love her, Colly, you know," he said, and then he laughed. "And as you said, I'm not getting any younger, so I'd better hurry up. Seriously though, we don't see any point in waiting any longer. It's going to be a quiet wedding here with only the immediate family and you, Pat and Tom. It will be good to have us all together. I wouldn't want to get married without you all there. I must be getting soft in my old age."

"I don't see any reason why not," answered Colly. "I'm really pleased and looking forward to the day."

At the end of the summer, they all headed off to Derry to watch Chris exchange his vows with Marie, and there was no one happier for them than Colly. She was glad he had someone to look after him, and someone to belong to as she belonged to Pat.

They stood and watched them drive away on their honeymoon, and it felt as if everything was changing for them all. Life was moving on and nothing could ever be the same again.

Chapter Fifteen

In bed later that night, Pat turned to Colly and said, "Things are changing, sweetheart."

"Yes, I know," she replied. "I had that feeling all day myself."

"And we are going to have to change with them," Pat said.

"I have also come to that conclusion," she replied.

"There is something I have to tell you," he said seriously.

She looked at him questioningly.

"I've been asked to a meeting with the big brass, in my capacity as a Republican solicitor, to discuss the implications of the British offer of talks with the IRA. It could mean the end of the conflict. Maybe we can find a peaceful solution to the war in the North," he said.

"I assume you will go," she answered. "We've spoken about this before, and we know we will have to think of other options now rather than what we've been doing."

"Yes, you're right, and I am going. I have to give them my reply some day next week, and they will let me know the details later. I think it is imperative now that we talk to the British if there is to be any hope of an end to this. I don't like it and I don't trust them, but we have to try," said Pat tiredly.

"I know," replied Colly. "If there is a glimmer of hope at all, we have to try it. This war has been going on for too long. We are all tired."

"What about Tom?" she asked after a while.

"I'm not going to tell him," Pat said. "From the way he is thinking at the moment, he will probably tell me I'm a traitor."

"Maybe it's best for now that he doesn't know," she said. "Perhaps nothing will come of it."

They both knew that it would take a miracle to get Tom around to their way of thinking. Neither knew what would happen to him or what he would do if the IRA decided to agree to peace talks or called a ceasefire. They did not want to think of what his reaction would be.

At the moment, all of that was in the future, and when or if it happened, then they would worry about Tom. Now Pat knew he had to put all of his energy into what was immediately important, and that was trying to create dialogue with the British, no matter how little he trusted them.

Colly's life took on a different slant around that time, with the easing off of her own active involvement. Pat, her children and work became top of her list. It was as though her personal crusade had come to an end. With all her might she had fought for years for what she believed in and still believed in. But now she was tired, and the final result was yet to be seen, and she hoped that it would come about without more bloodshed.

Her belief that their activities, and those of the rest of the Nationalist and Republican paramilitaries and supporters, had brought the situation in the North to its present state was firm in her mind. Her conviction was that if she and others like her had not put the pressure on the British by bombing their buildings and attacking their military personnel, the Catholics in the North would still be living under the oppression of the cruel Loyalist ruling hand.

She was convinced totally that the English would not have done anything to change the situation if they had not been made to by the actions of the IRA. Now they were beginning to realise that they could no longer close their eyes to the wishes of the Catholics in the six counties. From now on, she knew that they would have to consider the opinions of the Nationalist people, no matter what their policies or decisions would be in the future.

She also knew that the English could not just up sticks in the middle of the night and leave Northern Ireland. No matter how much it stuck in her throat, she understood that the Loyalists' views would also have to be taken into consideration by them.

All that mattered now to her was the final result and how it was achieved. She hoped it would be peaceably. A united Ireland was what she wanted and always would; future methods of achieving this were still in the melting pot.

Chapter Sixteen

Life became, for the first time she could remember, what she could describe as normal. Working very hard and commuting between Belfast and home with Pat was a regular pattern. The unit was not officially disbanded, but their activities were at a minimum. Sometimes it seemed as though it was long ago and in the past. Pat and Colly would spend weekends away relaxing, and she had begun to stop worrying about him.

On reflection, she could not remember a time when she had not been fighting for justice in Ireland. From when she was a child, it had been her number one priority.

When she was a child, she had fought her imaginary battles alongside Chris. Later it was through the civil rights movement, and from then until that day, she had been actively involved in the unit.

I'm tired, she thought. *Let someone else take up my banner. It's their turn now. Selfishness is going to be my motto from now on. My leisure time is going to be spent pampering myself and Pat, and spending time with the family.*

Pat said she would probably take up another cause now that she had finished with this one. He told her that it was in her blood to fight for justice.

But lying in bed, she dreamed of spending her days with him in peace. Although she dreamed, she knew that the reality could be very different. There was a long way to go, and it was not going to be easy. There had been so many splits in the Republican organisations and if the peace talks ever became a positive option, she believed there would be more. No way would all the Republican supporters be persuaded that talking with the British was the way to go.

Nor would the Loyalists be persuaded that they could be ruled by Dublin with the rest of the thirty-two counties, and all ties with Britain cut.

History was a painfully imbedded wound in the Nationalist psyche with the reneging of promises, cruelty, trickery and starvation by the British. It was so greatly ingrained that it would take more than a few promises to remove. But that was something that would have to be worked at, and it was as yet only in its embryonic stage.

As Colly lay in bed one morning nestled in Pat's arms, she could hear the birds twittering in the trees as a glint of the first rays of the morning light came through the curtains – she was pondering over this sleepily. She breathed a prayer to her Nan, as she usually did in the morning, in thanksgiving for keeping her friends and herself safe up until now. She also asked her to look over them in the future.

Pat sometimes laughed at how fervently Colly believed that her Nan was looking after her. She didn't mind, she knew if it was at all possible, then that was what she was doing.

As she stirred, Pat said, "Colly, are you awake? I need to talk to you."

She turned and looked at him.

"What's the matter?" she said. "You sound worried."

"I am," he answered. "I heard yesterday that there is to be a big movement of arms from the North to the Republic. The Loyalists are changing tactics and are stepping up their activities. They have decided to target the towns on this side of the border, and are moving their guns and ammunition over to this side within the next week or so. They are getting very worried about the talks too."

She felt a strange sensation in her stomach and she realised that it was fear. Months had now passed since any of them had been on active service. Chris and Marie were happily married and were back in Donegal. He was enjoying the normality of life like the others, this with the exception of Tom.

Tom would come up with different schemes every now and then for them to carry out, but up until now Pat had persuaded him not to proceed with them. He had not been too happy with this but the arguments from Pat had been pretty convincing, and he had agreed to wait.

Pat had a contact that he had met at college who had been in the UDA. He was now out of action due to ill-health, but still kept in touch with his ex-comrades. He was a Protestant whose mother had been a Catholic brought up on the Falls Road. Her family had moved to Dublin at the start of the Troubles, and she had met her husband, who was a Protestant from Armagh, and married him there. No one in Belfast knew this, and when her son joined the UDA, it was assumed that both his parents were Protestants. Luckily, no one checked on either of them.

It was the same old story of divided loyalties. His mother had related the hardships of her life and those of all the other Catholics on the Falls Road while she had been growing up. The inequality and discrimination they had endured at the hands of the Loyalist people had a huge impact on him. Talking to Pat about the activities, he thought he was just passing it on to someone with Republican beliefs, but Pat always thought it was his way of changing the order of things, although this was never discussed. As he still had mates in the UDA, he had access to a lot of information others wouldn't have.

When he heard of any operations or movement of arms, he got in touch with Pat and warned him. The information was then passed on to the relevant people and they would change their plan of action, get the target out of the area or set up an ambush for the Loyalists. Pat said that he was a brave man who was fighting the war his way, the only way he knew how. So far, he had been totally reliable.

The others believed in Pat and trusted his judgement, and they knew he would not let them down. The information had helped save the lives of many important Republican members over the years, and the IRA had got some big caches of guns from this information. Other raids produced smaller booty, such as Semtex and other explosive material.

It always created the desired effect by increasing the Loyalists' awareness that the IRA knew what they were up to, and this really bothered them. It created dissension in the Loyalist organisations and stopped them from running an efficient operation.

But Colly knew that this time it was different. They would have to act on the information to prevent carnage from occurring in the towns on the Donegal side of the Border. It was inconceivable that they would do nothing to prevent this from happening.

"I've been informed that arrangements are now underway for the Loyalists to transport the arms and bombing material and that it will happen within the next week or so," said Pat. "We are going to have to make plans on how to deal with this. I have spoken to Chris, and I'm seeing Tom tonight."

"Damn it," said Colly. "I thought they had learned their lesson when they lost their other cargo to you in the last raids."

"I know," said Pat, "but we have to make sure that they don't succeed with this. It could be our town that is targeted, or your children or our friends that are killed or maimed this time. It has to be stopped."

"I just wish it was all over!" she replied.

"Maybe it will be soon," he answered hopefully. "Let's hope that the English are serious this time about finding a lasting solution to the problem. Unfortunately, they seem to be blowing hot and cold at the moment." Then he added, "There are talks going on quietly, and we think the Loyalists got wind of it, and that is why they are moving now."

"Is there ever going to be an end to it, Pat?" she asked tiredly. "Are we ever going to see peace and a united Ireland?"

"I hope so, my darling," he answered. "We have done all we can, and now we'll just wait to see if the others do the rest. After this, I am hanging up my boots. I believe I have to. We can't expect our luck to hold out forever. I feel myself getting more jittery with each operation we undertake. I can't go on like this. I need some normality in my life, and I need to live for us. I think I'm getting too old."

"That's what I want too, but when you've lived like we have for as long as we have, it is hard to get it out of your system," Colly answered. "I sometimes feel guilty that I'm not as involved as I was, even though common sense tells me to let go."

"That's why Tom will never let go – he can't," said Pat. "If he did, the guilt would kill him. He feels as we do, but he will never trust the British or Irish governments to find a fair solution to the problem, and he will always feel the same. We know we have to let them try, because we are no longer creating the impact we desire with our present methods."

"Good luck to them," said Colly, "they are going to need it. Roll on, the next few weeks, until this is all over and we can settle in to a nice mundane lifestyle. I'm really looking forward to it."

Chapter Seventeen

Psychic was not a title Colly would have labelled on herself, but a strange foreboding came over her in the following weeks as the unit prepared to launch their attack on the Loyalists. She questioned the others repeatedly on every detail of the operation.

Pat would try to reassure her that everything was in hand, but she still worried.

"Don't worry," he told her. "Our contact hasn't let us down yet, and we have all the information we need to carry out a successful seizure of their cargo."

Every minute part of the operation had been gone over diligently as the information came through. They discussed how they would manoeuvre the cargo from north to south. Tom was occupied day and night surveying the terrain they would be going over. He had sorted out a secondary escape route if anything went wrong, had watched the military patrolling the area and knew their every movement, and had worked out the most advantageous point to create the ambush.

The details of whether they should plant a remotely controlled bomb on the road to blow up the truck or go in for a surprise attack from some vantage point were gone over time and time again, weighing up the pros and cons. The men checked the guns. They were using three AK-47s.

At one point a mortar launcher was considered, but was dismissed due to its unreliability. Finally, they settled on blowing up the lorry at a strategic part of the road by first putting in place an obstacle which would ensure that the truck stopped. The obstacle would have to be movable and look natural so that it wouldn't raise suspicions in case other traffic came along that route. This was unlikely as it was in a very backward area. Nevertheless, they couldn't take the chance. One of the men would install himself further up the road to watch for the lorry and give a prearranged signal to the others when he saw it approach. Tom agreed to do this, and he would take his binoculars with him, and a whistle to give the signal.

Nothing had been left to chance as far as the unit was concerned. All they had to do now was to wait for the word that the move was definitely going ahead, and when it was going to happen. That came one evening when Pat and Colly were at home alone. Pat took the phone call and told Colly. Then he journeyed to Tom's house and collected Chris on the way. They were all waiting for the go-ahead and had made arrangements to be in close proximity and easily contactable.

When she realised it was definitely happening, Colly could not settle. She tried walking in the countryside even though it was pouring rain. Sleep was out of the question. She decided to get outside and do a bit of exercise to burn off some of the restless energy she was generating.

She had tried to force Pat to take her with them, but he was adamant that she shouldn't come. She felt so scared. Never before had she felt like this. Maybe it was Pat talking about being jittery that was influencing her mood, but she couldn't shake it.

At one point she was going to follow them, but realised she couldn't do this as she knew that the men would not be impressed. She would be putting them, and herself, at risk.

It wasn't as if I don't know the drill, she thought. But she knew she was being silly.

She had been on enough training courses to know the dangers and the precautions that had to be taken, and that going in late to an operation was not a viable option.

"At least if I was there I would know what was going on," she worriedly murmured.

She waited and waited. The night came, and there was still no sign of the men.

"Damn it," she said, "they should have been back hours ago. Something must really have gone wrong."

She put on the radio at six o'clock to listen to the news, and she heard the newsflash which sent her into shock. It said that there had been a terrorist bombing incident in the area where she knew the men had gone. At least two people had been killed, and others were injured. A truck had been blown up, and a large consignment of arms had been found at the scene.

"Oh no!" she cried. "Please God, don't let it have been any of my men!"

She prayed that they would still be alive, even if they had been captured. She could live with that, as long as they were alive. The night was spent pacing the floor. She dozed for a while at around six o'clock the next morning, but was wide awake again when the clock rang seven.

What am I going to do, she thought. *I can't ring anyone to find out what has happened or send the Gardaí out looking for them. Yeah! That would really be great*, she thought cynically.

"What would I say?" she mused. "Maybe something like, "Excuse me, Garda, my partner and some friends went out to bomb a lorry full of guns that the Loyalists were shifting south of the Border, and they haven't come home yet. Could you tell me which of them were killed or injured?""

No! I definitely can't do that. It would be drawing attention to us if I asked anything, she thought.

The problem remained. What could she do? Nobody knew that Pat or the others were involved in these activities except for the chosen few, and Colly didn't know how to get in touch with them. She was going to have to wait. She thanked her lucky stars that she was on her own and that the family were all away. She would never have been able to explain to them why she was in such a state.

She felt guilty that she was praying for Pat to make it home to her more than for the others. She knew she would be devastated if anything happened to Chris or Tom – especially Chris. He had been her best friend since she was a child, but life without Pat would now be unimaginable.

She paced around the house, starting to do something, and halfway through, she would forget what it was she was doing and start something else.

As the one-thirty news came on, she heard the back door slam open, and the sound of voices and then someone running away. She rushed out to the back hall to find Pat staggering around. As she reached him, he collapsed onto the floor. His clothes were covered in mud;

and on his sleeve and coat, there was a lot of caked blood. By rolling him onto the floor mat and pulling and tugging, she finally got him as far as the range. He was soaked through.

She stripped him of his wet clothes and covered him in blankets, and then checked his wound. It was definitely from a bullet, but it had gone straight through the outer skin of his arm. He also had many bad gashes on his body. He had lost a lot of blood and this was the reason he had passed out.

Colly didn't understand how he had even made it this far without collapsing long before. Taking a basin with hot water and antiseptic, she began to wash him. He was gradually coming around.

Eventually, he opened his eyes and said, "Am I in heaven?"

"No, my darling, you are very much on earth," Colly smiled.

"I feel bad. I must be going to live." He smiled and grabbed her hand.

She got him to drink some hot tea to try and warm him up some more.

Then he closed his eyes and drifted off to sleep for hours. Keeping a vigil over him, Colly wondered what had happened to the others. She would have to wait until Pat woke, and then she would ask him. There was nothing either of them could do now, and whoever left him at the back door would know what was going on.

Ringing Marie was out of the question as Colly did not know if she knew about the operation and she would not be able to explain why she was inquiring, or what the outcome of it all would be. The less questions asked now meant less to be answered later when the full story was clear.

Pat opened his eyes a few hours later.

"Have you heard from Chris?" he asked, when reality hit him.

"No," replied Colly. "Where is he, Pat? What happened? Is he alright? Where are they? Did they both get away?"

"Colly! I'm so sorry," he said. "Tom didn't make it. The bomb went off but it only knocked the lorry on its side. The men in it tried to take the guns out of the lorry and put them into the two cars that were following. Tom lost his head and went charging in. He shot at least two of the others. We started shooting to draw their fire, but it was too late and we saw Tom falling. One of the Loyalists stood over him and shot him again. Then they started to shoot at us. I got hit as Chris and I turned to escape, and one of the bullets grazed Chris on the shoulder. We kept going though.

With all the mayhem, we became disorientated for a while, and we decided to stop and try and get our bearings. By this time, we had travelled over some very rough terrain. I had some bad falls because it had got dark. Then we remembered Tom's instructions about the second escape route so we retraced our steps, listening out for any movement in the area. I knew of a man who is a good IRA supporter in the area who would help us, so we called to his house. He drove me in his van to your back lane. He hid me under sheep fleece. It was him who left me here. Chris is staying with him and is being looked after. It was too dangerous for both of us to travel together. He will be safe. He will ring later. He had rung Marie with some excuse about work so she wouldn't worry. I insisted on coming home. I knew you would be worried sick, and I had to see you. I felt that if I made it here, everything would be alright."

She felt so relieved to have him with her, and to know that Chris had survived. She was very shocked and saddened about Tom.

"Poor Tom," she said. "We will miss him so much."

"I don't know what came over him," said Pat. "He could have got away. He knew that the bomb would have been heard for miles, and that the security forces would have arrived within a short time. The others would not have gone far with the guns. Some of them were injured from the blast. But he just charged in. It was so unlike him, he was usually so calculating. Did he want to die? Could he not face the future with the way he could see it was going?"

"I don't know," answered Colly. "Let's just be glad that you and Chris are safe. I'm really sorry we have lost Tom. I think you may be right, this was his way of ending his campaign."

Later, when they thought of it, all came to the same conclusion – that it was the ideal death for him. He died fighting for the country he loved and he died a hero. He would never have been happy to let the politicians decide on the future of Ireland.

His funeral took place a few weeks later. Both Pat and Chris's wounds had healed well, although they were still a bit stiff and sore, but both were very grateful to be alive. The three knew that this spelt the end of their active involvement and they accepted it, but they also knew it was not the end of the struggle. There was a long way to go and all of them would hang in there to see what the outcome would eventually be. Pat and Chris would go to the talks table and try and work out an eventual solution. Nobody knew how long this would last, or if all the Republican organisations could be held together for the duration, but they had to try.

Tom had left his farm to the three of them with the stipulations that it should be used to take young people out of the cities in the North and to show them a bit of their own country. They all thought this was a great idea and were in the process of developing a business plan for it. Tom was given a full Republican funeral with the tricolour over his coffin. The three of them attended together. They didn't care anymore whether they would be closely associated with him. They had loved him and he had loved them, and they had to be there in the end for him, to say their last goodbyes.

They left the graveyard together with their arms linked and their heads bowed, each with their own private thoughts and memories. They were going home to get on with life. They were still friends and would remain so, but they had decided that their war with the bomb and bullet was over.

They were going on to God only knows what lay in their futures.